TRAVELER

Dedicated to the memory of my brother,

Lloyd A. Lettis, Jr.,

an avid reader of science fiction.

TRAVELER

JAMES LETTIS

CITIOFBOOKS, INC.
3736 Eubank NE Suite A1
Albuquerque, NM 871113579
www.citiofbooks.com
Hotline: 1 (877) 3892759
Fax: 1 (505) 9307244

Ordering Information:

Quantity sales. Special discounts are available on quantity purchases by corporations, associations, and others. For details, contact the publisher at the address above.

Printed in the United States of America.

ISBN13:   Softcover   979-8-89391-339-2
             eBook   979-8-89391-352-1

Library of Congress Control Number: 2024919743

table of contents

chapter one

"Traveler"

The old man was trail weary, and looking for a place to rest. His leg, wounded in the attack, was swollen and continued to throb with a dull pain. The scorching sun overhead beat down mercilessly as he struggled to move forward. Shade was what he sought, but shade was scarce along this stretch of the stone wall he was following as a guide. The wall ran parallel to a dried-up river bed along the bottom of a long, narrow valley, with high barren mountains framing the desolate valley on either side.

In the five days the old man had been walking since leaving the Lake Clan village, he had not come across another living soul; nor had he expected to. His trade was that of a guide, and other than the few young men he guided, he shared this vast, hot, mountainous country he wandered through with few others. The eight little villages of humans he moved between were isolated by vast distances.

As unlikely as the event might be, the handful of others that plied the old man's trade would occasionally encounter one another on the faint trails they traveled. On this extremely rare occasion, they would pause to share any news they had gathered, before continuing on their way. In all his considerable rains of wandering, the old man had encountered fewer than a handful of others. The country was so vast and empty it had been well over ten rains since he had last seen another human on the trail, other than those he guided.

The old man did not know the name the ancients had given to the country he roamed; nor for that matter, the continent, or even the planet. That knowledge was lost to the ages and had ceased to have importance to those few fortunate souls whose ancestors had survived the Great Change. The catastrophic event that occurred many hundreds of generations in the past, that left a lasting curse on the human race for all eternity. But, regardless of their small numbers, the few humans that now somehow survived in this harsh environment and inhabited the tiny, isolated villages, still considered themselves to be the lucky ones; the chosen ones; or simply as they called themselves; The People.

On this particular journey the old man was traveling alone, which in itself was highly unusual. No young men accompanied him to carry his pack, and his ancient body was feeling the effects. Like most of The People, the old man's body had deformities. Combine these deformities with the fact he was extremely old, he struggled under the weight of his pack. However, the old man was driven by an urgency, some irresistible force, compelling him to reach the next village as soon as possible. So he struggled on.

As was his father, grandfather, and hundreds more before him, the old man limping along the dusty path in search of shade, was also a storyteller. He was known to all who knew him simply as Traveler, and he knew no other name. Traveler claimed allegiance to no clan, though many claimed him in theirs. As a storyteller, he was the keeper of The People's history since the written word had also been lost to the ages. But, Traveler was not just a gifted storyteller, he also served the village clans he traveled between in other unique capacities. He carried what meager news he acquired on his visits between the villages, and the villagers were eager to hear. They were especially anxious for any news from their relatives and that involved the old man's last, and perhaps, greatest service to The People.

It was the custom of The People, for young men to seek a mate from another clan, and Traveler arranged such unions between the various isolated clans many rains in advance. He was first the matchmaker, and later the guide for these young men journeying to their new village where their prearranged mate awaited.

Measured by the passing of the rainy seasons, Traveler had already seen forty and eight, or forty and nine rains, if his memory served him correctly. Of course he could be wrong, it might very well be more, but he was confident it wasn't less. Either way though, amongst The People he wandered between he was old; indeed, very, very old. In all of the storytellers vast travels, he had encountered only one other member of The People that had lived to claim as many passing rains. She was a dear old friend, known to all as Mother, and Traveler was presently heading her way.

Mother was a member of the Rushing River Clan, and if she still lived, Traveler was in need of her wisdom. Other than just being a dear friend, Mother was also a Seer, highly revered for her prophecies and wisdom throughout the land. The old man was having disturbing shadow visions while he slept and he was searching for answers.

In the past few rains of wandering, Traveler's chosen profession was becoming increasingly more difficult to perform. He was acutely aware of the fact his body was slowly wearing down, since he could easily feel it with every step he took. He was certain his shadow spirit's time to make the journey to the Spirit World was rapidly drawing near.

Like all of The People, Traveler believed his fate was predetermined by the God's, and he had no say in the matter. His days on the Real Side were limited and he doubted he would see another rain's passing. Still, the old man accepted his fate and was not overly concerned, for dying was a part of living. He acknowledged with grateful thanks, each new dawn as a gift from Mother Earth and Father Sun, while also embracing the knowledge that each new day of life also brought him one day closer to being reunited with the love of his life, Cel, in the Spirit World. He was supremely confident that Cel, as well as their three children, would be waiting to greet him when his shadow spirit passed over to the Spirit World .

Traveler's brow furled in concentration as he strived to bring his loved one's image to his mind. He had been alone far too long, with the passage of many, many rains, since Cel had left the Real Side and passed over to the Spirit World. His memory of her face had faded over the many rains and his mind was beginning to play tricks on him. He did remember Cel had a crooked smile and a sagging eye, but to Traveler, she had always been beautiful. The old man had thought in the past it was her left eye that sagged, but now he wasn't so certain. Recently, his mind occasionally felt as if a heavy morning fog engulfed him, adding to his confusion, and blocking out all sense of direction. These episodes would leave him terrified with thoughts that he was losing his mind. His memory had even deserted him entirely for short periods of time, before just as suddenly clearing back to normal.

'Was his mind playing tricks on him; somehow funning with him.' He could think of no other explanation.

The old man recalled a couple of moons ago, his confusion had been so acute that he wandered for two full days in the wrong direction, only to wake on the morning of the third day with a clear head; unsure of where he was. With the help of the surrounding mountain peaks, he eventually regained his bearings, realized his mistake, and found the little village he was seeking. The two young men he had been guiding at the time were terrified as well, fearing their spirit's time in the Real World had come to an end and they were certain to pass over to the Spirit World.

With this recent occurrence still fresh in his thoughts, Traveler was not surprised that Cel's image would no longer materialize in his mind; no matter how hard he concentrated.

Even though he desperately ached to see her face again, he was still quite certain he would be able to recognize her in the Spirit World. He was also very curious to see what kind of men his two sons had grown to become. *'And, what about his daughter? Had she grown to be as beautiful as her mother?'* Traveler remembered briefly holding each of his tiny baby's deformed bodies, before suffocating them against his chest, in the Shadow Spirit Dance as tradition required.

After limping a little further along the stone wall, Traveler finally found a suitable place to rest. The spot he chose was in the partial shade of a large, dead, banana tree. He carefully removed his carved, wooden eye-slit with his good hand, dropping it to dangle on his chest, held there by the small leather cord looped around his neck. Using the back of his withered and curled hand, he wiped some of the sweat from his brow and attempted to rub the trail dust from his eyes. He then turned and used a corner of his soft ratta leather shoulder cape to finish wiping the sweat from his face with his good hand.

He stiffly eased his tired body down to rest. The knee on the leg of his clubfoot complained, with its customary jolt of pain, as he bent to sit. Traveler grimaced with the pain as he settled down to lean against the lichen covered stone wall. The banana leaves were dead and brown from the heat, but it was still a blessing to sit a spell even under what little shade they cast. He looked closely at the blackened soles of his feet, and with his good hand removed the remains of a big thorn he found on one. The soles of his bare feet were darkened and trail hardened from endless journeys and the thorn had been but a slight irritant.

Even with the filtered rays of sunlight penetrating through the banana leaves, the sun's glare was becoming painful to Traveler's sensitive eyes, and he quickly replaced his eye-slit. Like other members of The People, his eyes were much better adapted to the dark. More than just the sun's glare, it annoyed him no end that his eyesight was slowly deteriorating as well; growing dimmer over the last ten rains or so. He now had great difficulty seeing anything up close. When he thought about his failing eyesight, he had always been quick to dismiss it, for he had already seen far more than any others he knew. He always told himself, *'Why worry about something that cannot be changed?'* Lately though, he was growing more and more concerned. *'How would he continue to wander if he could not see? What use would he be to The People if he could not wander? Would just being a storyteller be enough value to a village, or would the village elders step in and decide on a different fate?'* Those were all questions he was now asking himself. Questions with no definitive answers.

If he was forced to choose between banishment or suffocation, he would much rather be suffocated. He had plenty of friends that could assist him. Traveler knew suffocation was accepted and common amongst The People, especially for the elderly who were becoming a burden. At least, suffocation would be fast, and his spirit would have the added assistance of the Shadow Spirit Dance in passing over to the Spirit World. Traveler wondered, '*Is that the fate the Gods had determined for him?*'

Carefully leaning his worn, polished, staff against the stone wall, Traveler slipped his pack from his good shoulder. He shrugged his shoulders a few times to loosen the knots he felt in his shoulder and back muscles. He had not carried a pack in many rains, and had forgotten how heavy the rock-that-looks-back was.

Traveler pulled the soft ratta leather cap from his head and slowly walked his callused fingers across the top of his bald, wrinkled head. His finger tips abruptly found what they were searching for and gently began to massage around the edges of the large open sore. It was probably just wishful thinking on his part, but the old man thought the sore's edges felt a little less tender today. Certainly not the fiery pain of just a few days ago. After probing the sore's open center, he held his finger tips up close to his eye-slit for a few moments, before then smelling them. He was satisfied that the sore had finally stopped oozing blood and pus, but the odd odor still lingered on his finger tips. Knowing there was nothing else he could do at the moment, he carefully replaced his leather cap.

Traveler next began to examine the wounds on the ankle of his clubfoot. He nervously untied the two leather cords holding the dressing in place with his good hand, before gently unwrapping the medicinal leaves that covered the wounds. He examined the scarred leg, focusing on the two new gashes he recently suffered on his ankle. He was relieved that they both appeared to be healing nicely, for he knew from experience that infection was his biggest concern. Looking closer he saw no unusual redness surrounding the wounds. He was still a little worried though, since the gashes still pained him considerably and his ankle had been throbbing since the midmorning sun.

Traveler thought about the attack in the stunted brown nut tree two nights ago, as he rebound his wounds. He knew he had been fortunate to survive. The stunted tree had been hard to defend, but he had no other choice, for in this arid valley there were few trees. The battle with the attacking ratta had been exhausting and unusually long. With his ankle beginning to throb, his urgency to get to Mother's village for proper treatment was increasing. If his memory wasn't funning with him again, Mother's village was in the next valley over; just one more pass to climb. He knew he was getting close, and anticipated arriving in the village after one more sleep.

Traveler now had little doubt that Mother still lived. Somehow, he sensed it. Her shadow vision had appeared to him again in his dreams just last night, as if she were somehow beckoning him. Hopeful she could help, both with his shadow visions as well as his physical ailments, he was eager to reach her village. The thought of being reunited with the love-of-his-life in the Spirit World, with this stinking open sore on his head, was making him feel anxious. He hoped Mother would be able to heal it before his shadow spirit's time to pass.

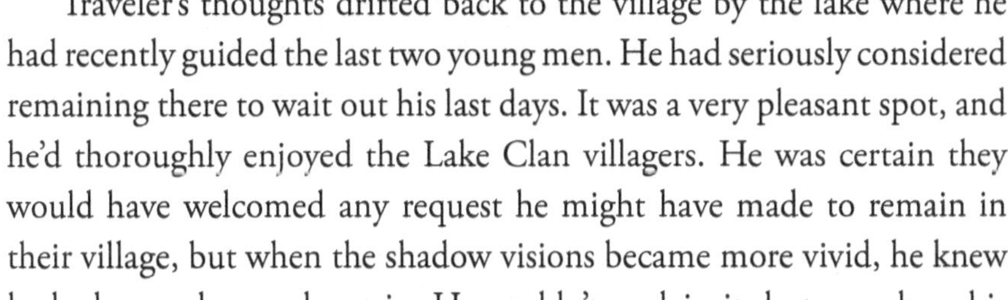

Traveler's thoughts drifted back to the village by the lake where he had recently guided the last two young men. He had seriously considered remaining there to wait out his last days. It was a very pleasant spot, and he'd thoroughly enjoyed the Lake Clan villagers. He was certain they would have welcomed any request he might have made to remain in their village, but when the shadow visions became more vivid, he knew he had to make one last trip. He couldn't explain it, but somehow his mind felt Mother's pull.

Since there were no young men in the village of proper age to seek their mate, Traveler had set out on this one last journey alone. He thanked the villagers for their hospitality and left at first light the following morning. He didn't anticipate the difficulties to come.

After a day's walk up the valley Traveler turned west and began to climb. It took him a day and a half of steady climbing to reach the break in the rocks, marking the summit of the mountain pass. He recalled when he was younger, this climb had been an easy half day's effort. When he stood at the summit and gazed out over the distant mountains, he was once again disappointed. From this high vantage point, he had anticipated seeing the source of his nightly shadow visions; a smoking mountain top. But, as had been the case in previous vantage points, it was not to be. None of the mountains in sight helped shed any light on the answer he sought. The smoking mountain of his shadow visions was not in sight.

After that disappointment, Traveler had to turn his thoughts to a more immediate problem, water. He had not been overly concerned when he reached the summit with his lack of water, for he had been thirsty many times in the past. He knew the location of a little weeping spring halfway down his descent from the pass and he murmured a quick prayer to Mother Earth concerning the spring.

She obviously heard Traveler's prayer, for when he reached the spring it still held ample sweet water. Even though the tiny spring only seeped from a small crack in the cliffside, a basin of sorts had been chipped and scraped out over the millennium from previous wanderers and the basin was full. He had been able to drink his fill, and refill his two empty water bags. Like other wanderers, Traveler knew there was another spring located a little less than a day's walk away, but that would have taken him in the wrong direction. He was happy that diversion had not been necessary, and he had taken the time, as always, to thank Mother Earth for her benevolence.

Traveler was very confident in his knowledge of all the water sources over the vast area he roamed, but he could never be certain any water he found would be sweet, and not sour. If he were to travel again he thought it might be a good idea to trade for another water bag when he reached Mother's village. He was moving much slower now and seemed to drain his water bags considerably faster. But, all that would have to wait for now.

As he rested, Traveler again began to feel very nervous about the next spring he sought, located at the far end of the arid valley he now walked in. More times than naught, that spring had been dry, or worse yet, sour in the past. He tried unsuccessfully to push these concerns to the back of his mind, but they would not go away. He told himself he would deal with it when the time came, but his fears lingered.

Traveler was certain there had been a shorter route to the Rushing River Clan's village, but he couldn't seem to bring it to mind. He exhaustedly looked at the lichen covered stone wall which he now found himself leaning against. It was solid and stood at least three times his height, a formidable barrier for sure. Even in the few spots where the stones had partially collapsed into great piles of rock, it had been many rains since he, in his limited physical capacity, would have contemplated climbing over, so he hardened his mind to the task ahead. He saw no other alternative but to walk on.

The sun sank another hand in the sky, and still Traveler continued to rest with his back against the stone. He withdrew the soft water bag from his pack, removed the wooden stopper, and took a short drink. He had been rationing his water and the ratta stomach water bag was almost empty. One more drink, maybe two at the most. His water situation was becoming dire. He had already drained his other water bag the night before. Again, he mulled over his options in his mind, but he remained confident in his decision.

His hand absently reached back into his pack and searched for any dried berries, nuts, or dried ratta that might still be lingering there. He pushed aside the rock-that-looks-back at the bottom of the bag as he searched. Traveler's face gave a small grin as his fingers closed around two brown-nuts. He withdrew the large nuts and cracked them on the black rock surface he had been walking on with the heavy end of his staff. The first nut was full of the little webs of the brown nut worm, but he found a small part of the nut still uneaten. He used a large thorn from a nearby dried-up cactus to dig out the remainder of the nut, and along with the plump worm, popped them both into his mouth. The second brown nut was a little shriveled up, but it still tasted good.

Traveler gazed up through the dead banana leaves to better judge the sun's remaining light. He didn't bother to search for bananas knowing this was not the right time. They appeared on the trees three moons after the two rainy moons that made up the rainy season. Still, his mind couldn't help envisioning a bunch of small, yellow bananas. They were one of the rare treats he looked forward to after the rainy season. Like many of the other fruit trees, he knew the location of most of the banana trees in the vast land he wandered.

Traveler's thoughts turned back to the wall he leaned against. He ran his good hand over the lichen covered stones in hopes of finding any lichen still suitable to eat. He found none, but he really didn't expect to. The lichen were all withered and dry from the intense heat and lack of water.

It had been at least three rainy seasons since Traveler had last traversed this particular valley. Having wandered untold numbers of valleys since, his memory had forgotten how numerous the stone walls were. He had walked along many walls in turn, always hoping for an opportunity to squeeze through any gap that might adjust his travel more to the direction he sought. So far he had been unsuccessful in finding gaps, but twice the stone wall he had been following came to an abrupt end, giving him an easy opportunity to adjust his route of travel.

The storyteller focused his attention on the larger, base stone's size. He had often marveled at the stone wall's height and mass. Traveler was certain, few, if any of the villagers he knew possessed the strength to lift even the smaller stones in the wall, much less budge the larger ones. His father had surmised long ago that the walls had been constructed by the giants. The ancient ones from the past; the ones Traveler knew from the stories. However, he never could understand the stone wall's purpose, for he was quite certain the walls wouldn't keep the ratta out.

Traveler knew all the stories concerning the giant humans of the past. At least all the stories his father and grandfather had passed down to him. The giants were thought to be distant ancestors of The People, who had lived many, many, hundreds of generations in the past. So long ago that very little was left from that previous time, although Traveler's father and grandfather both felt certain, the stone walls originated all the way back to that time. Maybe even the mysterious smooth black rock paths he walked on as well, that ran along many of the stone walls. Back in the time before that terrible day when the sky burned, the earth shook, and the cities crumbled.

Traveler came out of his thoughts and glanced quickly around. He could see the shadows were stretching longer from the stone wall and nearby cactus and it was time to move on. He started to lift the water bag to his mouth before thinking better of it. He pushed the carved wooden stopper back in place and returned the near-empty bag to his pack. Pushing himself up with the assistance of his staff, Traveler reached back down for his pack. He flung it over his aching shoulder and, out of habit, looked around for the four legged companion he called Scar.

Scar had mysteriously disappeared five moon's ago, when he was guiding two men to a far northern village. Unlike Traveler, his four legged companion had been completely hairless. The beast's shoulders had stood level with those of his own, and she could have easily killed him if she so chose. They had been wandering the paths together for many rains and he was saddened to think their time together might have abruptly come to an end.

Occasionally, Scar had left Traveler for a few days at a time, but always reunited with him on the trail later. This time was different. Scar had never been gone for this length of time, and the old man was worried, missing her dearly. He had questioned the two young men who were accompanying him at the time of her disappearance, but both denied having had any type of altercation with the beast. Traveler knew most of the young men he guided were scared of Scar so he had no reason to doubt them. If they had antagonized her, they would probably be dead, for she could easily rip their throats out if she had felt threatened.

Out of habit, Traveler gave one last, shrill whistle for the beast, knowing beforehand, that his wish would probably not be answered. He genuinely feared for her fate. Maybe the ratta had caught his companion, or Scar had been seriously injured and her shadow spirit had passed over to the Spirit World. In either of those likely scenarios the ratta would have feasted on her remains. Unlikely as the case might be, perhaps she had rejoined her wild pack. He hoped so.

Traveler turned his thoughts away from Scar for the moment and started back on his journey. The old man's clubfoot was a finger or two

shorter than his good leg and this gave him an uneven gait as he walked. With the assistance of his staff, the old man slowly picked up his rhythm and speed, and the dull ache in his ankle, knee, and shoulder returned. Pain had become a persistent companion for Traveler, but he knew if he turned his thoughts elsewhere, the pain would soon work its way to the back fringes of his mind. As he concentrated on his stride, his mind slowly reverted back to the dreamlike state which allowed him to both dull the pain and cover the monotonous distances he trudged each day.

chapter two

"The Sky Burned and the Earth Shook"

A **volcano rumbled in the distance**, quickly followed by a slight, side to side shudder of the ground upon which Traveler walked. This jolt caused the old man to momentarily stumble, but he quickly recovered with the aide of his staff. Ground tremors were common in the land, almost a daily occurrence, and posed little concern to the storyteller. Mother Earth was probably simply rolling over in her sleep.

Traveler was still well aware of his surroundings and was hoping to reach the next spring before the coming darkness forced him to seek the safety of a big tree. That is, if he could find one. He was exhausted and didn't want to have to battle the ratta again from a stunted tree.

As he continued walking, Traveler began to question his decision to leave the lake village in the first place. If he had stayed, he could have lived out his last days in leisure. Instead, his shadow vision had compelled him to seek out Mother. He questioned whether she could even help solve the shadow vision. He didn't realize the difficulty of wandering without the help of young men, as well as the danger. His ankle was a clear reminder to the old man that the danger was real as it continued to throb. The pain wasn't overbearing, but it was constant, and Traveler was well aware that it could have been worse.

The old man's daydreams again circled back to the forested valley with the beautiful lake he had recently left. It was entirely different from the valley he now traversed. The faint path he presently followed was hard and rocky, offering sparse shade. The old man had been crisscrossing the length and width of this parched valley for the last two and a half days now, following where the black rock paths and stone walls allowed him.

Often he had difficulty following the faint trail as it weaved around numerous small mounds of flakey, reddish-brown rock located on this section of the hard, black rock path. These mounds were often covered with thorny thickets of dried-up berry vines. The mounds had always puzzled Traveler. Most of the mounds were similar in size. Sometimes close together, while other times well spread out, but they were always located on the wide black rock paths. If the flat black rock was truly a path of the ancient inhabitants as his father had believed, why would they leave piles of flakey reddish-brown rock on their path? Why would the black rock paths need to be so wide in the first place? Could the ancient ones really have been such giants as to have need for such a wide path? Neither Traveler, nor his father, could ever come to a satisfactory answer. It was a puzzlement to both of them.

Walking these trails was a challenge for an old man with one arm and a clubfoot. Besides avoiding the reddish mounds with their thorny thickets, Traveler had to skirt numerous clumps of cactus that had pushed up through the black rock's cracked and broken surface. Occasionally, the black rock path itself was interrupted by deep, steep walled, washed out gullies. Searching for a safe spot to cross a deep gully was time consuming, and time was a luxury the old man didn't have to waste with water running low.

As Traveler searched for a safe spot to cross each of these gullies he was also on the look out for breaks in the stone walls, which might allow him to shorten his route. Few opportunities presented themselves that he thought he could safely negotiate. Caution was a priority, since any serious injury alone in this arid valley, would lead directly to the Spirit World. Climbing down and then back up through the numerous gullies left the old man near exhaustion as it was. Once, when he couldn't determine any other alternative, Traveler even had to push his way through a patch of unforgiving cactus, which tore at his arms, feet, and legs.

Along any path he traveled, the shade of an occasional stunted brown nut tree offered some welcome respite from the blistering sun, but unfortunately Traveler had only encountered a few growing along this stretch of the black rock path. Staring ahead, the exhausted old man saw nary a tree in the distance which concerned him. The blazing sun, stone wall, and black rock path remained his only constants, and he struggled on. He had no other choice.

Traveler knew he had passed this way many times before, but without the help of the young men he guided, the path seemed to have grown longer and more difficult. His shoulder, knees, and ankle continued to ache. He bent over and picked up a small pebble to suck on as he walked. His father had taught him this trick as a small boy to help alleviate thirst, and he had been doing it ever since when warranted.

Trying his best to block the thirst and pain from his mind, Traveler began to reflect back on his life's journey. He had not known his mother, who's shadow spirit had passed over to the Spirit World shortly after giving him life; trading her life for his. The old man thought a moment as he limped along, but could not even recall his mother's name. He remembered his father had often spoken fondly of her, but Traveler would have to make her actual acquaintance in the Spirit World.

Other than losing his mother, his life had been a simple, good one. He started wandering with his father after six rains, when his uncle deemed him old enough and strong enough for the challenging journeys. His father immediately began to teach Traveler The People's stories. The stories were the history of The People, passed down from one generation to the next. Of course he didn't believe some of the stories, but he dutifully memorized and repeated them exactly as his father had instructed him. Now Traveler had to find someone worthy to pass the stories and the walking staff down to, and he was running out of time.

All three of his own children's shadow spirit's had passed over to the Spirit World with the help of the Shadow Spirit Dance. He had not been able to save even one, despite all his best efforts. Traveler had been unable to summon forth the right words necessary to convince the Head Man of any of his new-born's birth-worth. Their deformities had all been more severe than his, so perhaps the Spirit World had indeed been the more logical choice.

His mind, though disappointed, was now at peace with these decisions. Traveler took heart knowing the decisions meant his children had not had to face the Real Side's many hardships. The old man was getting impatient to learn if his children had become story tellers in the Spirit World. After all, his father and grandfathers were all there to instruct his children.

Traveler often wondered what words his father had spoken in order to convince the Head Man of his own birth-worth to the tribe. With a club foot and withered arm and hand, most new-borns in his birth condition would have passed over with the help of the Shadow Spirit Dance. Somehow his father had found the necessary words to save his son's life. Then again, the old man thought, maybe his Father had nothing to do with it. Perhaps the Gods had a special reason for sparing his life? Was it his destiny to do something special? Something like the Wise One? He thought a moment about the Wise One and then scoffed at the idea that he too was somehow destined for greatness. He walked on as the sun blazed down from above.

As he walked, Traveler studied the stone wall. His thoughts turned to the ancient humans, drifting back to the ruined city he had once seen early in his wanderings. He must have been eight or nine rains old when his father took him to see it. His father had just finished telling him the story of the cities destruction and had asked Traveler if he wanted to see one. Traveler excitedly said he would and they had set off early the following morning. He remembered walking south for three long days, sleeping safely high in the brown nut trees at night. On the morning of the forth day, not long after their trek had resumed, his father abruptly stopped, and signaled him to kneel down and remain quietly where he was. When his father returned, he led Traveler to the top of a nearby hill. Crawling up the final short distance to the crest, the two slowly raised their heads and peered down upon a crumbled city.

At first, Traveler did not comprehend what his father was showing him. To Traveler, the ruins looked like endless piles of stones, brush, and what appeared to be, large reddish-brown tree stumps sticking out at various angels. When he asked his father what could have broken off such large trees, his father quietly whispered that they had not been trees at all, but a mystery from the past. His father said the reddish-brown stumps were hard as stone and could not be cut. Not even with the hardest black-flake axe. His father assured him he had once tried.

Traveler's father told him there were many other crumbled and ruined cities throughout the land, mainly to the South. As he lay there staring down at the ruins below, he began to think about the story his father had recently told him, regarding the ancient city's demise. He tried to visualize in his mind what it must have been like living in this city when Princess Blue's lightning bolts began to rain down.

Seeing how the ruins continued as far as he could see, Traveler also thought about the story his father had told him of the great numbers of ancient giant humans who once lived in these ruined cities. Ever since he saw the vast ruins in person Traveler's mind puzzled over the story. Of course, he knew the story well, but seldom retold it for it was so unbelievable that he had no answers for the many questions that always followed its telling. He had given this story long, serious thought and was totally perplexed. On one side, Traveler had seen the vast ruins with his own eyes, but he always ended with the same question. *'What could so many people possibly eat? Especially if they were giants. There weren't enough ratta in the whole valley to feed such a gathering; even for a couple of days.'* Since Traveler's mind could not comprehend such a thing, he simply seldom recited the destruction story. Yes, he knew it. He knew them all.

While he laid looking down on the crumbled city, his father had tapped him on the shoulder and pointed his staff in a slightly different direction. Traveler sighted down his father's staff and caught a glimpse of a hideous looking, powerfully built, creature slowly moving over the broken stones. The creature paused now and then to listen before moving a stone or two. It was clearly hunting something.

The large creature cautiously moved about, walking a little stooped over, but still on two legs like The People. Traveler was certain it stood easily three or four times his father's height. A thick layer of dark fur completely covered the creature's back side, from the top of its head, down to its feet. Except for a black patch of fur covering his genitals, the front side of the creature's body was bare. *'Could he be actually looking at one of the ancient humans? The giant humans that built the stone walls?'*

The creature's movements became even slower as it continued to hunt. Finally, it stopped and slowly knelt down. It remained motionless for a long time, turning his head side to side before lowering his ear closer to the stones. Seemingly satisfied, the creature suddenly flipped a huge stone aside, and jabbed a hand down between the rocks. That's when Traveler was shocked to see, what appeared to be, four of The People spring forth from their discovered hiding place and flee in multiple directions only to vanish again into the rocks. Ignoring the fleeing others the beast slowly withdrew his hand from between the rocks, grasping its unfortunate prey by one leg. The giant held his struggling prey up close to his face, seemingly studying its victim, before violently swinging downward and dashing his captive's head on the rocks. The creature again held the limp body high and let out a chilling, triumphant, scream before turning and vanishing deeper within the ruins.

Even now, thinking back, the memory of what he had witnessed with his father gave him chills. He was certain the creature's prey had been one of The People, not much bigger than himself. It was then his father had given him a stern warning, *'Never venture near the ruined cities again, son. Promise me, never again.'* To this day, Traveler had not broken the promise he made those many years ago to his father; nor had he felt any desire to do so.

Since that day, many, many rains ago, Traveler had learned from another wanderer of the existence of two additional ruins, many days walk farther to the South. Considerably farther south than Traveler had ever ventured. When Traveler asked the wanderer, the man said he had not seen any life, but acknowledged he had heard strange screams in the night. He likened them to the screams of demons, and the man had been too frightened to investigate the sounds by entering the ruins. He had felt the presence of many shadow spirit's, and he cautioned Traveler, like his father had beforehand, to give any ruins a wide berth. *'Something truly evil lurks there.'*

As he continued to walk, Traveler's mind left the image of the ruined cities and drifted to the story passed down explaining their destruction. He had recited this story many times in the past. The story revolved around two of the most powerful Gods of The People; Mother Earth and her daughter, Princess Blue, the Sky Goddess.

The story tells of an angry and resentful Princess, who blamed her mother for favoring the humans over her birds. She had complained to Mother Earth for many generations that the humans were killing her beautiful birds, and pleaded with her mother to step in and do something. Each time, Mother Earth had simply smiled and shrugged her shoulders, saying there were plenty of birds and sarcastically mocked her daughter's request. *'What would you have me do child, kill the humans?'*

Mother Earth continued to do nothing and the birds continued to die at the hands of the humans. Until one day, a human killed Princess Blue's favorite bird; a beautiful white swan. This infuriated the princess and she went into an uncontrollable rage. If her mother would do nothing, she would take matters into her own hands. Princess Blue would have her revenge. She began to rain lightning bolts down upon the human's cities, hurling one after another in an angry fury; unleashing her wrath upon the humans, guilty or not. Within minutes, the cities quickly turned to ruins under the deluge of lightning bolts.

Mother Earth was too slow to intervene and was furious at her daughter's defiance. With a rage of her own she would punish her out-of-control daughter. She would teach Princess Blue a lesson she would never forget. Mother Earth called upon her volcanoes to awaken. The earth violently shuddered with each great boom as all her volcanoes began to erupt at the same time and spew forth their lava, fulfilling

Mother Earth's command. The heat of the eruptions was so intense that it set the sky aflame, and killed all the birds.

When the Sky Goddess realized what Mother Earth was doing, she stopped hurling her lightning bolts at the cities and begged her mother to stop. *'Please, mother, don't kill all the birds.'* But, by then it was too late. The cities were all destroyed and the sky was aglow in a dull red. Princess Blue's beautiful birds were all dead.

When Mother Earth's anger wained and she finally heard her daughter's pleas, she too stopped; but it was too late. Looking around, Mother Earth realized the carnage they both had caused. Earth, her greatest creation, lay in ruins; destroyed in a fit of anger. She banished her daughter from earth for a generation before collapsing herself, from shame and exhaustion, into a deep, fitful sleep.

Of course the sky darkened with the banishment of Princess Blue, the Sky Goddess, and a deep, shadowy gloom fell over the land. The darkness lasted the whole generation of Princess Blue's banishment. It was only when the princess finally returned did the sky brighten again to its original blue. The princess was shocked to find her mother still asleep. She tried her best to awaken Mother Earth, but to no avail.

Mother Earth's slumber was not a peaceful sleep; not at all. She often would twist and turn in her sleep from unpleasant shadow visions, causing the ground she lay upon to shudder. Occasionally, if Mother Earth's shadow visions were vivid and unpleasant enough, a volcano would reawaken to spew forth it's lava.

The volcanos Mother Earth had originally unleashed did not stop when Mother Earth fell asleep. They continued to spew forth their molten rock and gasses, until the lava was finally exhausted after a period of two moons. During the time of eruptions the air temperature steadily rose throughout the land. Most plant life unable to adapt to the drastic change in heat and gases died off. A few others seemed to flourish. As certain plants died, so did the animals that depended on them for food. Only those few animal species that could find adequate shelter were able to adapt, and survived.

It is said that Princes Blue remembers with sadness and deep regret, each anniversary of the day she became enraged and destroyed the cities. She visits her sleeping mother that day and sits by her side for a period of two moons. As she sits by her mother's side, Princess Blue weeps with remorse over her role in the earth's destruction. To this day, her tears pour forth over the land for the period of two moons; the time the sky burned and her beautiful birds died.

The four seasons of the earth's past were reduced to two; constant summer with stifling heat, and the two moons of rain being the only variation. The rainy moons very quickly became The People's reference point in keeping track of a person's age or other important events; commonly referred to as 'rains.'

chapter three

"Ratta, Soarers, and Humans"

The stories passed down from generation to generation also warned The People that the lakes and rivers held their own terrors, and should be avoided if at all possible. So the villagers did so as best they could. The clans lived in such strict isolation that any knowledge they once had of the great oceans, rivers, and mountains of the planet they lived on had been totally lost to them over the generations.

There eventually came to be three dominate animals species in the lands inhabited by The People; ratta, sky soarers, and humans. With the human population, at first, dominated by the other two.

The ratta and the sky soarers were the two species able to adapt with ease and immediately began to flourish. They grew larger, and larger, and then grew some more. The ratta now stood as tall as a man's knee. To better regulate their body temperature in the stifling heat they developed a thick layer of fat, and lost their hair. They continued to live in their underground burrows and only emerged to hunt at midnight, when the temperature had dropped a few degrees. For a long time, they feasted in the ruined cities as scavengers. At first they ate everything but over time, they became ever more fond of rotting, human flesh. For an extended period of time, there seemed to be an endless supply. Over generations, the ratta grew bolder, and bolder and became more of a hunter rather than a scavenger. The primary prey they sought continued to be humans; dead or alive.

The great soarers also came from the caves. Out of necessity, their main prey became the multitudes of ratta. Ratta were smaller than humans, easier to catch, and far more abundant. Over countless generations as the ratta grew in size the soarers naturally grew as well. Their leathery wings could now open as wide as a human could stretch his arms. From the tree tops, Traveler had often observed the soarers hunt in the moon light. They rode the hot air currents, silently circling before swooping down on their prey from above to kill with talon and teeth. They were deadly killers.

Of course, ratta was the staple food of humans as well; if they could catch one alone. Eventually, the sheer numbers of the ratta drove the surviving humans from the caves and tunnels and forced them to seek refuge in the trees. Living in the trees the humans were relatively safe since adult ratta had grown too large to climb the trees. The younger ratta however, still could, and would always make the effort.

Besides the few ratta they could kill, humans lived on fruits, nuts, plants, roots, and insects. Over time human bodies slowly adapted to their environment as well. Because of the many generations of living in the caves and tunnels their eyesight slowly adapted to the dark. Most humans lost their hair, although a few still had small tuffs randomly located about their bodies. They became smaller of stature because of their inadequate food supply and better adapted to moving amongst the tree-tops. Their fingers, toes, and arms grew a little longer in order to assist them in moving about in the trees. And, birth deformities became the norm.

Human's continued to forage at night because of their changed eye sight, but this brought them into closer contact with the ratta and soarers. Fire-hardened spears and stone clubs were always carried when the humans descended to forage for food on the ground as night fell. They always were conscious of the nearest tree. Still, the ratta swarms made a meal of the unwary or slow reacting human who stayed on the ground too long.

There was seldom any trouble between humans and soarers. But, before the humans moved down from the trees, if a parent were not vigilant, an unguarded baby would occasionally be plucked from a tree nest by a hungry soarer. In times of great hunger, all the creatures turned to cannibalism, and the humans were no exception.

chapter four

"The Wise One"

The stories say, The People did not come down from the trees for multitudes of generations. Not until one boy, forever known in The People's oral lore as the Wise One, was born. From an early age, the Wise One began to observe the world around him. When he was just eight rains, he observed that ratta feared any type of rushing water, never venturing near, not even to drink. They only drank from still pools, and then approached very cautiously. He surmised that perhaps the ratta had grown too heavy to swim. His insight was tested when he captured a young ratta. When he dropped the ratta into water, it instantly stiffened with shock and fear, before sinking to the bottom and drowning.

With this knowledge, the Wise One encouraged his friends to help him prove his observation. He proposed to dig a channel to divert some of the river water. The channel would surround a small stick hut he would build on the ground, before flowing back into the river. It would be a huge project to complete. The Elders tried to talk him out of it, telling him he would be sacrificing himself needlessly. But, the Wise One was so certain of his theory, he would prove to The People that water would indeed protect them from the ratta. This channel had to be dug during the day when the ratta slept, and that presented, yet, another problem; the blazing sunlight.

The Wise One, once again, put his mind to finding a solution. He observed that when he squinted his eyes, the intense sunlight did not hurt as much. But how could he continuously squint his eyes? He then carved the first eye-slits for he and his companions to wear. Wearing the eye-slits, which covered their eyes and had a narrow viewing slit, they were able to cut down the sun's glare and work during the day digging the water channel, unhindered by the ratta.

This channel took many moons for the young boys to accomplish. There were times they had to ward off the river terrors with spears and clubs, but finally a portion of the river was successfully diverted. The river terrors were prevented from entering the channel by lashed wooden grates where the channel and river joined. Most importantly, none of the boys had passed over to the Spirit World during the channels construction; at least, not yet.

Still, the elders remained skeptical. Not until the Wise One lived in the hut for a whole moon without incident, did their opinions change. The Wise One proved to The People that the ratta indeed, would not cross the running water in the channel. They no longer had to fear the ratta in the dark and they gradually descended from the trees.

The word spread slowly from one small group of humans to another, but they all quickly adapted. Through trial and error, they learned how to carve the wooden eye-slits. Eventually, elaborate channels were dug around new fields and newly constructed villages. Two or more water channels became the norm. Diverting the rivers into channels had a secondary effect as well. They made it easier to water the various crops the villagers grew. The crops were grown within the outer water channels and the villages were constructed within the inner water channel. As the villages grew larger, additional water channels were added to expand the fields and increase The People's food supply.

Lastly, the Wise One showed The People how to build the tip-board traps. The traps were ingenious in their simplicity of design. A wide, flat piece of wood was carved with pivot posts in the sides near the board's center. The boards were then polished smooth so the doomed ratta could not grab hold. Once the tip-boards was secured to the side boards of the trap by their pivot posts, the front half of the side boards were pegged securely on the outer bank of the outer channel. The trap's other end was suspended over the water channel, held in place by leather strips attached from the side boards to a tree. The bank side of the tip-board would hold the ratta's weight, but the side of the board over the water was unsupported and would suddenly tip downward when the ratta passed the board's pivot point. This action would drop the doomed creature into the rushing water channel below. To overcome the ratta's natural fear of rushing water, woven side panels were added to the traps a short distance on either side of the trap's entrance. These tightly woven panels kept the animals from seeing the rushing water as they approached the traps.

Now the traps had to be baited.

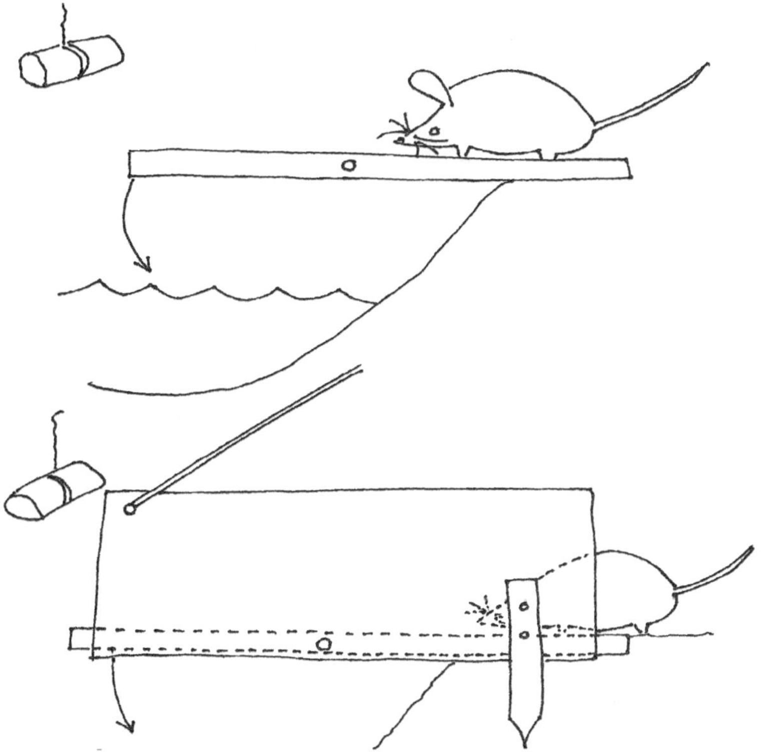

The Wise One drew pictures in the sand to help explain the tip-boards to the villagers.

To this day, ratta simply cannot resist the desire for rotting, human flesh. This has been bred into them through countless generations. A piece of rotting human flesh was carefully secured to dangle above the far end of the traps, just beyond the tip-board. In the dark of night the ratta would come, attracted by the bait out onto the tip-board. The boards would then tip the ratta into the water. The villagers only had to harvest their daily supply of drowned ratta that washed up against a cane screen a little way down the channel.

The tip-boards were an instant success. Ratta may be big and mean, but they also were not very bright. The villagers were ecstatic with a ready supply of meat.

These three things changed The People's lives forever. They quickly learned to tan and use ratta hides for shoulder capes and head caps to protect them from the scorching sun. They melted down rich, ratta fat to make candles. Ratta stomachs were used to carry water. But, most of all, the villagers feasted on the rich meat of the ratta itself. One adult ratta would easily feed a large family.

The few bands of nomadic humans, not near adequate running water to dig a channel, joined other villages that had a good water source. They stopped their nomadic ways. The new villages were able to raise their squash, beans and corn without the worry that the ratta would eat all their hard work in the night. If the tip-board traps were properly baited they were always successful. Even though there seemed to be an endless supply of ratta, the villagers were careful to only trap as many as they needed. They began to preserve the meat with smoke and sun for the rainy moons when the ratta slept. The times of hunger diminished and The People began to multiply and flourish.

When the Wise One suddenly passed over to the Spirit World at the early age of fourteen rains, it was a devastating loss to all The People, not just his clan. He had been testing a new observation that went bad. The Wise One saw that the river offered the villagers an abundant source of food, if only it could be caught. He watched as the leaves and sticks easily floated on the water's surface. If there was a way he too could float on the water, he could then spear the great shadows that roamed just below the surface. He cut and bound three tree trunks together, to test his theory. Unfortunately, the logs broke apart when they struck a rock, and his flesh was lost to one of the very river terrors he was trying to kill.

<hr>

Traveler stopped for a moment and reached in his pack for his water bag and drank the last of his water. He had told these stories about the incredible gifts of knowledge the Wise One gave to The People many times, but the villagers never tired of hearing them again. These stories, and the ones about the incredible animals that lived before the Great Change were always asked for, especially by the young.

He glanced up to check the sun's position again. He still had one more mountain pass to climb before dropping down into the valley he sought. Even though the summit was not as challenging as the pass he climbed just a few days ago, Traveler knew he was too exhausted to finish the climb before nightfall. He was also certain the spring was close by, and he began searching for green. Any green vegetation in the area would indicate water. He climbed to the top of a small rise and spotted a group of green trees and vegetation just a short distance away. He had found the spring, but now, would the water be sweet or sour?

The small spring and pool of water it formed were surrounded by small trees, bushes, and grass. Traveler approached and began examining the muddy area surrounding the pool for animal prints. He was hoping that his lost companion might have been drawn to the spring, but the only prints of any kind were ratta. Lots of ratta! The old man poked the mud near the pool with the tip of the walking staff before kneeling down and taking a small sip from his cupped hand. A smile crossed his weathered face and he tried a second sip. To his surprise, the water was cool, clear, and sweet, and he mumbled a quick thanks to Mother Earth for her generosity.

Traveler wasted little time filling his two water bags and dropping them back into his pack. He then leaned forward and drank a long cool drink. When he had finished his drink, he submerged his face in the shallow pool, and splashed the cool water over his tired body. Scooping up a handful of the soft mud at the pool's edge with his good hand, he then began to rub the mud on his body to deter the little insect biters that lived near the pool.

When he had finished rubbing on the mud and relaxing at the pool for a while, Traveler began looking around for something to eat. He spotted a small group of wild onions growing in the shade of some brush a few paces from the spring. Traveler used his walking staff to dig them up. While rinsing the onions at the pool, he spotted a small patch of watercress growing on the far side. Dropping the onions into his pack, he gathered all the watercress he could find. At least he wouldn't go to sleep on an empty stomach.

Traveler pulled an onion from his pack and absently chewed on it as he turned his attention to finding a suitable tree in which to pass the night. Any tall tree would do, as long as he could reach a lower branch, but his preference was a brown nut tree with its wide branches. To his good fortune he found one close by. He was very pleased indeed. Compared to others he had seen in this valley the tree was a big one.

He scouted around beneath the tree for any brown-nuts the ratta might have missed. Unfortunately he found only broken shells amongst the leaves rotting on the ground, but he would not give up his search for brown-nuts that easily. He began to climb. Pushing his walking staff up before him he wedged it between the crooks of branches before using it to help him climb. Climbing trees had always challenged Traveler, and with his club foot, feeble arm, and now injured ankle, it was indeed a slow process. He knew, the higher he climbed, the safer he would be so he kept climbing. He wanted to be high enough so the young ratta could only attack from one branch. Traveler did not fancy the thought of being bitten again since he was already concerned about infection from his latest bites. If infection didn't kill you outright, it certainly could linger for many moons if it settled in.

The old man finally located a nice spread of branches high in the tree that he was able to bend to his needs. He quickly bent some small nearby branches and wove them into the shape of a small nest in which to sit. As he was climbing, Traveler had also searched the crooks of branches for any brown-nuts that might have lodged there as they fell. Although he had been hoping to find more, he was pleased with the three large brown-nuts he did find, and thanked Mother Earth, just the same. After all, three nuts were better than nothing at all.

As he swayed in the tree tops to a soft breeze, the old man used the walking staff to crack and eat the brown-nuts, and finished the wild onions and watercress, savoring each small morsel. He then settled back to sleep, confident from past experience, that he was safe for the moment. A cooling breeze gently swayed the tree tops, and Traveler quickly dozed off. He did, however, hold the walking staff securely on his lap with his good hand, ready to bash the first ratta of the night that he would encounter.

After a time, Traveler woke. From experience, the old man knew the ratta would be coming shortly. He absently rubbed the knob of his heavy walking staff. As the old man waited, he turned his hand-worn, polished, wooden walking staff in his hands. His thoughts drifted to his father, as they generally did when he stopped to appreciate his heirloom. He had once tried to determine how many rains the staff might have been through, but had found the task impossible. The walking staff had been a dying gift, passed down to him from his father when he was fifteen rains old. He also knew the staff had belonged to his grandfather, because his father had told him so. Probably his great grandfather before that, but beyond his great grandfather he could only surmise. Traveler just knew it was old, very old indeed, and it was one of two possessions he truly valued.

He was uneasy about what was to become of the staff when his shadow spirit passed over. '*Who could he gift it to on the Real Side? Who was even worthy of such a gift? Perhaps his shadow spirit would allow him to take the staff with him when he passed over to the Spirit World? Was that even possible? And, what could he do with the rock-that-looks-back?*'

The old man rubbed his hands over the odd shaped creature carved on top of the heavy staff. His father had called it a '*bird.*' One of Princess Blue's creatures that flew in the sky before The People were cursed. His father had told him a bird's body was covered by feathers. But, the concept of feathers had always troubled Traveler's mind. He could not visualize them, and his father could not really explain in more detail since, he too, had never come across an actual feather. Traveler ran his fingers over the carved shape. His father had told him that birds came in many shapes and sizes. The bird on his staff was indeed very small compared to the great soarers that roamed the skies of the present. The great soarers were the only sky flyers he had ever known, and they were creatures of the night.

As the old man had predicted, the attack came in the darkest period of the night. Traveler knew the ratta would find him, as they could easily track a human's scent. He was quietly waiting for them. He watched in the dead of night as they scurried excitedly around, sniffing the leaves at the base of the tree. He counted almost two handfuls, but he knew more would be bound to show up later. A few of the ones he watched below were much too fat to be concerned about, for they would not be able to climb. The others however, were now standing on their hind legs, loudly sniffing up the trunk of the tree with their long, whiskered snouts. As they leaned against the trunk, they suddenly stopped sniffing and began to peer up into the branches above. They were confident their prey was hiding somewhere above and their beady little eyes searched for the human's location. After a few moments, two ratta began to climb. They had spotted their prey, and were quickly followed by others.

The old man gripped his walking staff a little tighter in his good hand, ready to do battle. He was more annoyed than concerned, for this drama was not new. Rather, it played out nightly for all those who, like Traveler, chose to wander the vast lands beyond the safety of the village water channels.

Just as Traveler had planned, the ratta had no choice but to attack single file. If the ratta's prey had been asleep, injured, or too young to fight back, they would have been doomed. The ratta would go straight for the neck, slashing their victims throat with their long teeth and needle like claws. However, this was not the case in this encounter. Traveler was wide awake and waiting. He remained perfectly still as the first ratta quietly approached. Once the ratta was within easy striking distance, the old man quickly bashed it aside with the heavy walking staff. The stupid animals were not adapted to the tree tops, and out of their element. They were ground and tunnel dwellers, and easily lost their balance as the old man knocked them aside one after another. But, they were indeed slow learners. Others just kept on coming.

The ratta overcame their lack of intelligence and awkwardness, with shear determination and numbers. The first few ratta that fell from the tree tops, were uninjured and quickly scurried over to the trunk to climb again, not wanting to miss their share of the spoils. Others that Traveler dislodged were not so lucky. They were either injured in the fall or knocked unconscious by the old man's blow. The fat, slow ratta that had been patiently waiting, now saw their opportunity. They quickly attacked the injured or unconscious ratta that fell from above. The fight for survival now became fierce as other ratta joined in to bite and tear at each other. Traveler heard the snarling and fighting going on below him, as the ratta turned to cannibalism, and a grim smile of satisfaction crossed the old man's face. Traveler was also certain, the fighting below would likely attract a few of the great soarers in the area, who would also feast on ratta tonight.

Eventually the attack on the old man ceased and the surviving ratta disappeared into the brush as silently as they had come. The ratta had either eaten their fill of their unfortunate comrades, or wandered off licking their wounds. The attack had been similar to hundreds of others Traveler had survived, and he leaned back against the branches that held him, knowing he could now return to sleep undisturbed. As he closed his eyes and drifted off to sleep, he was hopeful that he might find one of the gravely wounded or dead ratta caught-up in one of the crooks of branches when they fell. He licked his lips as he thought about the possibility. *'That would make for a very welcome meal in the morning.'*

chapter five

"Bobane"

The following morning, Traveler did not find a dead ratta in a crook of branches as he had hoped for. As he searched the area under the tree, even the few bones he found had been cracked open and their marrow sucked dry. He turned his attention elsewhere and drank his fill of water from the spring. He then scoured the area for anything else he might eat, and eventually found some overripe cactus fruit still clinging to the cactus leaves. Carefully breaking them off with a stick to avoid the stickers, he then used his black flake knife to slice the fruit open. He ate the inside of all the fruit he found before cutting off a new, tender cactus leaf. Carefully slicing the thorns off, the old man stuck the cactus leaf and knife carefully into his pack before swinging his pack over his shoulder. Picking up his walking staff, he turned his attention toward the mountain pass before him. He was eager to begin the short ascent to the pass that would take him to the next valley where he was confident Mother awaited.

The climb was easy compared to the steep climb out of the lake village, but it still took the crippled old man most of the morning. Finally, standing in the pass, Traveler gazed out over a small valley, considerably different from the one he was leaving behind. The obvious difference was that this new valley had water. He could see the wide, gentle river that flowed down the valley's length. A broad swath of green vegetation and tall trees grew along both sides of the river's bank. Beyond this line of trees and shrubs grew an expansive area of head-high dry grass stretching half-way up the gentle slope he would soon descend. At first, Traveler's mind welcomed the greenness of the valley spread out below. Then his eyes focused on the numerous stone walls, running this way and that, in no particular pattern, throughout the valley. Similar to the stone walls that had been so numerous and burdensome in the valley he had just left.

The old man let out a long sigh as he sat, momentarily depressed, on a nearby boulder. After a short period of time, he took a deep breath. He reminded himself that this was the final challenge of his journey. He reached into his pack and carefully withdrew the cactus leaf. Using his black flint knife, he cut and trimmend the thorns from the leaf to reach the juicy, moist interior. as he ate, he studied the maze of walls protruding up through the tall grass on the valley floor. It didn't take the old man long before he was satisfied with the route of travel he worked out in his mind. When his meager meal was finished, he was ready to begin his descent to the valley below.

Traveler had just slung his pack over his shoulder, when the old man's eyes glanced up. He stared at the distant mountains rising beyond the far side of the valley. Perhaps two or more valleys beyond, it was hard to tell. He was initially stunned, while at the same time, entirely certain. The old man was staring at the same smoking mountain of his nightly shadow visions. The large volcano was significantly taller than the surrounding mountains and volcanoes in his view. A tremendous amount of white smoke was bellowing forth from its distant summit. He was surprised that he did not see this mountain in the past. Traveler continued to stare a short time longer, trying to comprehend what his shadow vision might mean. He was overcome with a sense of urgency as he started his descent. He had to speak with Mother.

Late in the afternoon, Traveler finally reached the tall brown nut trees that grew along the banks of the river. He welcomed the shade they offered as he walked amongst them and his pace quickened. The village had to be close because he could now hear the flowing water just beyond the stone wall he was following. Finally, the stone wall came to an abrupt end where a deep, dry, gully had washed it away during the rains. Probably the last rains, as Traveler noted some of the fallen trees still had a few branches of green leaves.

The old man carefully began to work his way down into the gully over the tangle of fallen stones and trees. When he reached the tall grass growing near the river he paused to search the area for one of the river terrors that may be in the area protecting a nest or just sunning itself. He saw numerous matted down trails in the grass, but no river terrors.

Satisfied that he was alone, he began to make his way through the grass and toward the river. When he finally caught a glimpse of the river and could see the far bank, he spied the top of one of the outlying mud huts, the field workers used as shelter from the midday blazing sun.

Traveler studied the fields and village across the river. Things had certainly changed since the last time he had visited, and not just the washed out gully. The fields on the opposite bank appeared to be much larger than he recalled from his last visit three rains ago. Satisfied as to his location along the river, the old man turned and began to walk upstream to the crossing which was at the base of the mountains.

He moved quietly and cautiously along the river, wary for any lurking danger on shore while maintaining a safe distance from the river's edge. Although he had drained his two water skins some time ago and was very thirsty for a drink, he dared not approach the water. He had already witnessed a water terror burst forth from a river's depths to devour an unwary youngster. He would wait for his drink.

Traveler had watched the sun dip a full hand when he finally approached the mountain's steep cliffs. Even though he couldn't see the crossing he sought, the rising mist and river's roar told him he was close to the crossing. As the river flowed forth from a narrow canyon at the base of the cliffs, the water was squeezed between two huge boulders jutting out from the cliffs on either bank.

Traveler marveled in awe at the sheer power, and volume of water violently being squeezed through the deep, narrow channel. The noise was deafening, and he welcomed the soaking he received from the cooling mist.

This however was not the crossing Traveler sought. Even with the river narrowing, it was still way too wide to pass. Traveler approached the huge boulder on his side of the river and was relieved to see the notched log still secure in place, leaning against the boulder. He quickly climbed up the log to stand on top of the giant boulder. The old man mumbled his thanks to Mother Earth when he saw the huge logjam of broken logs and limbs that had been trapped just upstream from the river's violent narrowing.

Mapping out each step in his mind beforehand, Traveler carefully climbed up and out onto the tangled logs. It was difficult for him, with his ailments and exhaustion. The logjam was made even more challenging by the rising mist from the river's violence below. The logs were wet, mossy, and very slippery. Traveler cautiously, made his way across the entangled logs, realizing all the while that one slip would plunge him to sudden death waiting just below.

Finally reaching the far bank of the river, Traveler let out a deep sigh of relief. He wasted little time climbing down the notched log leaning against the rocks and quickly began to make his way back to the village downstream. Perhaps too quickly. He was so relieved from not slipping on the wet logs that he somehow hadn't noticed a river terror sunning itself on a patch of sand a few paces from the bottom of the notched tree ladder. The old man watched the terror's yellow eyes follow his every movement as he gave it as wide a berth as he could. He thanked Mother Earth again when the great beast showed little interest as he passed. He admonished himself for being so careless.

Lucky for escaping such a violent death he grinned when he reached the first water channel surrounding the outer fields. Traveler had heard the village drums calling the workers in from the fields just after he had crossed the log jam, so he was pleased to see the two log bridge still in place. He quickly crossed the makeshift bridge before kneeling down by the channel's edge for a long, satisfying, drink from the fast moving water. Still kneeling, he raised his good hand and withered arm and looked to the sky to give thanks to Mother Earth for her generosity.

Once his thirst was quenched, the old man began to follow the narrow path through the village's outer fields. The drums had emptied the fields of workers and he was relieved to find the outer log bridge still intact. He certainly did not want to spend another night in the trees.

Traveler continued to pass through the deserted fields of well tended hills of squash and pumpkin, as well as rows of corn, tomatoes and beans. He had been able to block his hunger from his mind as he traveled, but seeing such an abundance of food, he now began to realize just how hungry he was. His stomach growled in anticipation of a coming meal. He was certain the villagers wouldn't mind, so he stepped into the nearest field and picked two ripe tomatoes from the closest vine.

He returned to the path leading toward the village, consuming the first tomato as he walked. He had not walked far when a group of men, coming from the direction of the village, approached him on the path. One immediately recognized who he was, and greeted the trail weary old man with open arms.

"Welcome, Traveler. It has been too long between visits."

"Yanni, it is with joy that my old eyes gaze upon your face again. I'm glad to see you are well," Traveler replied as tomato juice and seeds flowed down his chin.

"I see you still like to steal tomatoes."

"I was hungry! I hope you don't mind."

Traveler wiped his face with the edge of his cape and the two men hugged and clapped each other's back, as was the custom.

"We were just coming out to pull the log bridges to the village side of the water channels," Yanni said. "You're lucky, you made it in just in time. We were held up some leaving the village."

A few of them had already removed their eye-slits and they dangled on their chests on leather cords. Even though the sun had set and dusk was beginning to take hold, Traveler kept his in place.

Traveler laughed, patting the backs of the others as they each stepped forward in turn to great him with a quick hug. It was good to greet any of The People, since life was so fragile. An unknown boy stepped forward, dipped his head and eyes as custom demanded in the presence of one's elders, and offered to carry the old man's pack. Traveler gladly removed the strap from his shoulder and handed it to the boy.

Yanni looked beyond the fields before asking, "Where is that ugly, hairless beast that wanders the trails with you? The one you call Scar."

The storyteller just shrugged his good shoulder, shook his head from side to side, and lowered his eyes in response. The others were curious as well, but it would be bad manners to speak out loud of those who had passed over, even an animal. It was obvious that the old man was saddened by his loss of Scar, so nothing else was mentioned on the matter. If Traveler wanted to share something further, he would do so in his own time.

Traveler sat with the boy along the path while the village men went to pull the log bridges. After the outer channel logs of the bridge were pulled back, Traveler and the boy fell in line behind Yanni as the group made its way back to the village. They crossed two more water channels before entering the village itself. As the men crossed each channel in turn, the logs were pulled back to the village side of the channel. Once the last bridge had been pulled back, the ratta were no longer a threat.

As was the custom in villages of The People, the stick and mud, dugout huts were arranged in a large circle, around the head man's larger hut, within the circle's center. The entrance to each hut did not face this central clearing, but, they certainly were not random either. Each hut's entrance was aligned in such a manor as to be shaded from the rays of the midday sun. Just outside each hut's entrance, against the mud wall, was a fire pit lined with stones. They were only used for cooking and then quickly extinguished. There was no need for a fire's warmth in such a hot climate and wood was becoming scarce.

The larger Head Man's hut was off-set a little within the center of the circle of huts in such a location that its entrance did open onto the central clearing as well as avoiding the midday sun. The People gathered in this clearing each evening to dance, socialize, and discuss village matters. Such a circle of huts was important to maintain harmony and make each family group feel equal with their neighbors.

Upon hearing the approaching men's shouts and laughter, the villagers already in their huts began to emerge to see what the excitement was all about. Some were seeing a stranger for the first time, while others were seeing a cherished old friend. Both groups of villagers quickly began to chatter and gather in the central clearing, in front of the Head Man's hut.

Approaching the mud huts, it was obvious to Traveler that the village had grown since the last time he had visited. Perhaps even doubled. He counted in his mind more than six handfuls of huts in the circle. He knew it was customary for more than one family to occupy each hut, so a considerable number of people now resided here. Many men had multiple mates as well, which was also the custom. After walking through the expanded outer fields and now seeing so many huts the village appeared to be very prosperous indeed.

He turned to Yanni and asked, "The village has grown since my last visit. What has changed?"

Cautiously looking over at the men walking with him, his friend replied, "My Rushing River Clan invited the Smokey Mountain Clan to join them. We are one now."

"I am not familiar with the Smokey Mountain Clan," Traveler replied. "Where was their homeland?"

"I'm not certain. Only that it was far to the South."

As Traveler's growing group passed between the circle of huts and approached the central large hut, a tall man emerged from the entrance and stood stiffly, arms crossed in front of his chest. Traveler approached to stand at a polite distance before the taller man, as custom demanded. The old man was surprised when he did not recognize the tall man he stood before, as had been the case with many others from the village. With the tall man's stoic demeanor, it left little doubt that Traveler was standing before the village Head Man. He surmised the stranger must be from the Smokey Mountain Clan. Traveler wondered what had happened to his good friend Kia, the previous Head Man. The tall man grimaced sternly as he looked down on Traveler.

The two men took a moment to asses one another. Through his eye-slits, Traveler quickly wondered what he might have done to bring about the Head Man's obvious distain. He didn't think he had broken any customs and quickly dismissed the thought. He immediately noticed the tall man in front of him had no ears. Just small bumps behind his ear channels. Traveler didn't want to stare so he lowered his eyes downward and they were quickly drawn to the bleached white ratta hide cape, especially the beautiful picture of the sun above the mountains on the cape's left breast. Traveler wondered whether the sun was rising or setting, but the cape's stunning design and whiteness was very impressive nevertheless. The old man wondered how a hide could be made so white?

The Head Man also wore a well-designed cup of hide secured to the stump of his left arm. Traveler noted the man's hand was missing just above the wrist. Obviously, this was not a birth deformity; The People never covered those. The last puzzling item that caught Traveler's eye was a finely carved club hanging by a leather loop at the Head Man's waist.

A villager stepped up behind the white-caped Head Man and whispered into his ear. A wide smile slowly spread across the Head Man's face as he listened. He quickly took a few steps forward, spreading his arms in the customary greeting, but did not offer a hug. Instead, he grasped Traveler's shoulders and gently squeezed before stepping back.

"Ah, so this is the storyteller with the wild beast the villager's have spoken of so fondly. The rumor being whispered in the wind, was that your shadow spirit had passed over to wander and spread your stories and news in the Spirit World," the Head Man stated. "I'm happy, like most rumors, they were not true. You are, and will always be, welcome here. I'm certain the villagers are anxiously awaiting to hear your news as well as your stories." Looking around, the Head Man questionably added, "But, I don't see the incredible beast I've heard so much about?"

The same man, once again, quickly stepped up to the Head Man and whispered into his ear. The Head Man nodded his head in understanding as he listened and then raised his arms to the sky, in an acknowledgement of the Spirit World.

He lowered his arms back down and, once again, faced the storyteller standing before him. Nodding his head in understanding, he said, "Somber news, indeed. I am sorry."

Spreading his own arm wide with his own greeting, Traveler took a short step forward, slightly bowed his head in formal acknowledgement of the Head Man, and politely introduced himself. "My name is Traveler, and I claim no clan. I thank you for such a warm greeting, and I look forward to my stay in your village. The pathways I wander seem to be getting longer with each rain that passes. But, before I share my stories and news, I have a great need to visit an old friend. Does Mother still reside in the brown nut tree at the village edge?"

The smile vanished from the Head Man's face, replaced once again with a stern grimace. "I'm sorry Traveler, but that visit will not be easy. Yes, Mother still resides in the brown nut tree where she has lived with an assistant for, what I have been told, the last ten rains. But, unfortunately, Mother no longer welcomes visitors. She sees only her two great-granddaughters, who tend to her every need. Even I have never had the honor to greet her. Any visions she wishes to share with the village elders she conveys through her granddaughter, Violeta. As far as I know, Violeta is the only one allowed up in the tree in the last couple of rains. None of the villagers have ever even seen Emma, but Violeta assures us, her sister dwells in the tree with Mother. Violeta visits each morning, bringing food and water and what other needs they may have."

The Head Man shrugged his shoulders before continuing, "Perhaps, If you share with us what ails you, one of the villagers may be of assistance."

Traveler was still determined to speak with his old friend, but that would now have to wait. He did not want to mention anything about his shadow vision, for fear of alarming the village, so he did the next thing that came to mind. The old man gently removed his cap and tipped his head toward the Head Man. The villagers gathered nearby could see the old man's body and facial features were wrinkled and bronzed by the sun. Whereas, on the top of his head, the area protected from the sun's rays, his skin was considerably whiter. The storyteller slowly turned toward the gathering, tipping his head to reveal the large, open sore. A few of the nearby villagers, shuddered and held their hands to their mouths to keep from uttering something inappropriate. Some had seen similar sores in the past and the ailment was something they could not heal. As far as they knew, these flesh-eating sores lead to only one final outcome. One would have to be treated by a very skilled healer indeed, to escape death.

The Head Man looked about the gathered villagers before turning back to his guest. "I see no one has stepped forth with advice to what ails you. Perhaps Violeta might have overheard Mother speak of a treatment for such a sore in the past. I will send word that you wish to speak with her. I'm certain she will find you in the morning."

After the initial shock of seeing the celebrated visitor's ailment, the Head Man regained his composure to ask what many of those gathered were thinking. "May I be so bold as to ask, just how many rains you have seen, Traveler?"

Traveler knew this was an extremely rude and inappropriate question, but he displayed no offense. Many had asked the same. He replaced his cap, leaned on his staff, and quietly answered. "I have seen the passing of forty-eight rains, maybe forty-nine. I'm not certain."

There were audible gasps from a few of those villagers near enough to hear this astonishing answer. The others who already knew, just nodded their heads in agreement. Those who stood too far away to hear, turned to others for answers. Soon the gathering was talking quietly amongst themselves about what they had just heard. '*Could this really be true, or was this just one more of the old man's stories?*' Few in the village had seen the passing of half that number of rains, and they were still considered old.

Traveler quickly added, "You should not be surprised, Mother was birthing her first child when I began my wanderings with my father. She is many rains older."

The crowd slowly pushed in closer, both to better hear the soft spoken visitor, but also to get a better look at his wrinkled, bronzed hide. Most quietly stared, which was rude enough, but a few of the younger villagers that knew no better, actually reached out to touch the story-teller's leathery skin. They whispered amongst themselves that the old man's answer may indeed be true. Up close, the storyteller certainly did look old. From his withered arm and hand, to his sun-toughened, wrinkled face, they determined for themselves that, yes, Traveler must be very old indeed. Maybe not the passing of forty-eight rains though, that still seemed a bit outlandish. *'And, how could Mother possibly be as old as the storyteller claimed?'*

The Head Man suddenly raised his good hand in front of him, bowed his head a little, and apologized to his visitor. "I'm so sorry, Traveler, and please forgive me. We seldom have visitors, and I have not formally introduced myself. My name is Bobane, of the Smokey Mountain Clan. I am now the Head Man of this village."

Traveler was shocked at Bobane's introduction. "I did have questions when I did not greet my old friend, Kia. What has become of him? I have wandered great distances, but I have never heard of the Smokey Mountain Clan. Where did your clan last call home?"

Ignoring Traveler's questions for the moment the Head Man invites, "Please Traveler, honor my hut by joining me inside to eat with the elders. I will be happy to answer your questions as we eat. You must be hungry from your extended wanderings. The ratta we eat tonight is a gift from one of Mother's own grandsons, Moa. His gift of flesh baited the tip-traps."

At the mention of the grandson's name, the gathering all murmured under their breaths, "We give thanks to his shadow spirit."

This was the custom of The People and Traveler muttered the same words of thanks and respect. He remembered the young man and wondered how he had passed over, but custom prevented him from asking. Perhaps Mother would tell him when they spoke.

It was the accepted custom of The People that the flesh of the body was gladly given when the shadow spirit passed over to the Spirit World.

A person's shadow spirit would then be remembered with grateful thanks by all the villagers. The clans believed that once a person's shadow spirit had passed, the body left behind was just an empty, insignificant object. But, the actual flesh of the body was of great value and necessary for the survival of all. An easy gift to make for one's family and friends. For how else could the ratta be trapped? Ratta were mainly flesh-eaters, and the village had no other source.

Traveler leaned his staff outside, to the right of the hut's entrance, before following the Head Man in. He knew he would find his staff, as well as his pack, in the same location when he emerged. Like most crimes, there was no thievery among The People for the punishment was harsh; banishment! All were keenly aware that banishment meant certain death.

As he turned to enter the hut, Traveler first had to step up two steps and over the large packed earthen ring surrounding the hut. This ring prevented water from entering the hut during the rainy moons. Although shorter than most, even he had to stoop lower before pushing aside the hanging leather door flap and entering. Once inside he stepped down the traditional five steps to the earthen floor. This hut was the same as all the others he had been in, only much bigger. The ground had been dug out to the depth of his head, to take advantage of the earth's coolness. The removed earth was used to form the hut's surrounding ring. The roof was three times Traveler's height and made of poles and interwoven branches. The whole structure was then covered with woven reed mats, and then finished with a thick layer of mud. There was one large support post in the hut's center, with a smoke hole in the roof an arm's distance from the post. Of course, during most moons, the cooking was done outside in the shade of the hut. The People only cooked inside during the two moons of rain. Along the entire length of the circular walls, a low, wide, earthen bench was left when the hut was dug out. This bench was used for sitting as well as sleeping.

Traveler pulled down his eye-slit and let it dangle from his neck. His eyes quickly adjusted to the interior's darkness. He looked around to take in his surroundings. Two small oil lamps burned on either side of the central post. The old man had no difficulty seeing in the dark, and Traveler was astounded by what now caught his eye. On top of the reed floor matting on the hard packed floor lay a hide so massive that it stretched out to cover one entire side of the large hut. A hide so rare that, even he, an old man of forty-eight rains, had never seen another like it. When he ran his fingers over the hide he was astonished to find the hide was covered with fine hair. What type of great beast was this? Could this hide have come from an animal similar to the one Scar's pack had killed? In all of his wanderings he had only seen a few animal hides other than ratta, and, they were considerably smaller. Only one of those hides had tuffs of hair!

His mind remembered back to many, many rains ago when he and his father had caught a glimpse of a very large animal. It too had been in a northern forest. Traveler had thought at the time, he might have been able to walk under the four-legged beast without ducking. He especially remembered the bones sprouting out of the animal's head were huge. The majestic beast had probably sensed their presence because it had quickly moved back into the shadows of the forest, never to be seen again. Could this skin, lying under his feet, have come from a similar beast? Were they all of the same species that Scar's pack had killed?

Traveler rudely blurted out before being spoken to as tradition required, "What is this hide that covers such an area? Where did you get it?"

The Head Man smiled and replied, "Do you like it?" He continued, not waiting for Traveler's reply. "The two brothers who gave it to me were wanderers like you. Their father found the beast in a dark forest, far to the North. The creature's front leg was clearly broken, and its head, torn and bloody. It had obviously lost a ferocious battle. The man knew the ratta would swarm and feast on the crippled animal come night fall, so he assisted the injured beast into the spirit-world. He then took some meat and this hide as thanks."

"Did the men say anything about seeing great bones sprouting from the animal's head?"

"Not that I recall," replied the Head Man. "Why do you ask?"

"My father and I saw just such a beast at a distance many, many, rains ago. We as well were in a northern forest. Huge bones protruded from the beast's head," Traveler replied.

"Maybe, they were just a deformity," the Head Man suggested.

Traveler shrugged his good shoulder in reply, not knowing how to respond. "Perhaps," he answered a few moments later.

The old man ran his hand over the soft hide once more before standing and facing the Head Man. Furrowing his brow, he gave a little nod of his head in the Head Man's direction before questioning softly, "Why would one give up such a treasure?"

"I saved one of their lives from a river terror." Holding up his stumped arm the Head Man added, "This was the trade the river terror demanded. And this," moving his stumped arm over the hide, "was the wanderers' gift of thanks." The Head Man chuckled to himself before adding, "They later confided in me it was a huge burden carrying the thing around between them on a pole and they were glad to be rid of it."

The supper was served by two women; delicious strips of roast ratta, with onions, peppers and beans. Sweet melon was served last. Most of the elders finished their portions quickly, wiping the melon juice from their chins with their forearms before politely licking their bowl and hands clean. Each then loudly burped, as was the custom of The People, to show their satisfaction with the host's generous meal. Food was never to be wasted out of respect to those who offered their flesh so others might eat.

Even though the elders were growing impatient to listen to Traveler's news and stories, they waited patiently while the old man finished, quietly talking softly amongst themselves in the dark. After all, it would be rude to rush their guest in his meal of greeting.

Bobane ate a little slower. Finally, he set aside his half finished bowl, and turned to his quest. "You asked earlier about the death of your friend Kia."

The room suddenly grew quiet at Bobane's statement. "The previous Head Man, Kia, died quite suddenly shortly after our arrival. Tragically, he fell and hit his head on a rock while we were digging the new outer channel to expand the fields. I was working with him at the time of his accident, but did not see him slip and fall. He was a great man and his passing was unfortunate. I liked the old man very much. After all, he was very generous in offering the Smokey Mountain Clan aid."

Traveler stopped eating and sat quietly as he listened to the details of his old friend's death. Something felt odd as he listened. *'He was certain Bobane was leaving something out.'*

"As to your asking of where the Smokey Mountain Clan previously called home, we traveled from the base of the three smoking mountains, far to the South. It is understandable that you have not heard of us, for we walked a little over a full moon cycle to arrive here. We began our journey at the start of the rainy moons, three rains ago. We lost many friends along the way, before Head Man Kia was kind enough to offer us shelter, and here we are."

Bobane returned to his bowl and ate a few more morsels before setting the bowl aside again, still unfinished. He wiped his greasy fingers on the hide where he sat, and waited for his guest to finish.

Thinking about what he had just heard, Traveler resumed his meal, eating leisurely, savoring each and every delicious bite. It had been a while since he had had such a filling meal. After finishing a large slice of melon he slowly licked his wooden bowl clean.

Bobane and the elders continued to sit quietly, not wanting to utter a word that might slow the old man as he wiped the melon juice from his mouth and finished licking his fingers. They all waited patiently in anticipation of Traveler's burp. After what felt like an eternity, their guest finally set aside his clean wooden bowl and softly burped. The Head Man immediately followed with a loud burp of his own.

As if given some sort of formal command, the elders rose to their feet as one and quickly ducked out the hut's opening. They found their places on the hard packed earth within the inner circle of the village center. The waiting villagers, had already gathered in anticipation of the storyteller's tales, having formed a second and third circle around the elders. In a small area in the center of the gathered villagers, a small log had been rolled up next to Bobane's carved stump to allow the storyteller a place to sit.

Traveler finally emerged from the hut, closely followed by the Head Man. They both took their place, side by side, in the gathering's center. Finally, the stories began. The villagers sat spellbound as they listened to the storyteller's tales. Many of the stories they had heard before, but some were always new; especially to the young ones. And, Traveler knew many stories indeed, for he had lived a long life.

Between the stories, Traveler told the gathering the news from other clans he had visited in the last three rains. Villagers began to interrupt him to ask about specific relatives. The questions became so numerous that the old man grew a little agitated. He finally held up his good hand and told the gathering, it was not the time to ask about relatives. He would be more than happy to answer any personal questions they might have as he visited their huts in the days to come.

The stories went on well into the dark period, before Traveler yawned, stretched his good arm, and reached for his staff. As he began to rise, two elders quickly stepped forward to assist him. This was the storyteller's polite way of announcing that the stories were over for the evening. The villagers rose as one and turned to make their way back to their huts, chatting quietly amongst themselves as they walked.

The villagers couldn't hear the ratta rustling in the brush beyond the water barriers, but they could easily see the soarers in the sky, gliding silently overhead in the moonlight, searching for any ratta that might make a fatal mistake and wander too far from the brush. The villagers held their small children close, and they felt safe and happy as they made their way back to their huts.

That night, the village guest was honored to be invited to sleep in the Head Man's hut. Many others slept there as well, since the hut was large, but, there was plenty of space for the old man. He was especially pleased when he was offered a place to rest upon the strange beast's hide.

chapter six

"Shadow Spirit Dance"

Just before morning's first light, another shadow vision visited Traveler, disturbing his slumber. The shadow vision appeared in the form of a hunched-over old man, standing crookedly with the help of a walking staff. The vision was pointing to a smoking mountain in the distance. At first, Traveler did not recognize the shadow vision until the vision turned to face him, nodded his head twice, before slowly fading away. It was then, that Traveler knew the shadow vision's identity. Not from the shadow's face, but from the walking staff he held. The staff had a bird carved on its top so he knew the shadow spirit had to be his grandfather! He tried hard to bring the vision back, as he felt certain his grandfather was trying to tell him something. Something important, but Traveler did not understand. *'What about the smoking mountain?'*

Dawn broke beyond the darkness of the hut, as Traveler tossed and turned in the short time shared between deep sleep and waking. He drifted off into a sounder sleep when a different night shadow vision began to materialize. Once again, he did not immediately recognize the vision. Just a distant haze of a figure trying to work its way into his dreams. Suddenly, the shadow vision appeared directly in front of him, an arm's length from his face. It was Cel! The love-of-his-life was staring back into his eyes, as tears rolled down her face. Her left eye sagged as he now remembered. Her crooked mouth quivered, as she tried to speak, but her words came out garbled. Try as he might, his mind could not comprehend what the vision was desperately trying to say. *'She reached out . . .'*

Traveler was suddenly awakened by a muffled scream. His mind immediately tried to bring back the lost vision. What was the love-of-his-life's shadow vision trying to tell him? A second scream closely followed the first, bringing the old man fully alert. He rolled onto his stomach to rise from the hide and be of assistance. The hut's other inhabitants had been instantly awake with the woman's first scream. He now saw the Bobane pushing aside the leather flap and ducking out the opening, holding his club in his hand. He was followed closely by others. By the time the storyteller located his eye-slit and stood up, he was the last to emerge from the hut.

When Traveler finally pushed aside the hut's door flap and stepped out, he saw villagers beginning to congregate around a nearby hut. As he approached he heard the villagers whispering amongst themselves. The old man quickly learned there had been an unforeseen birthing during the night. The Head Man quickly ducted into the hut to assist the father with the delicate decision they now had to make. One could see the concern on the faces of the gathered villagers as they waited. Traveler overheard one woman whisper to another that she knew one of the women of the hut was pregnant but was not due to birth for another three or four moons. Traveler knew it was very unusual for a mother to cry out during birthing. That was not acceptable behavior of The People. He could see that the gathered villagers feared for the worst.

Everyone knew birth deformities remained the norm amongst the clans, ever since the Great Change. Deformities were the ongoing punishment the gods exacted for the horrific transgressions of The People's ancestors leading up to the Great Change. By custom, it was up to the Head Man and newborn's father to determine the infant's fate together. In reality though, it was the Head Man's decision, for it was unheard of for a father to challenge the clan leader. The Head Man made the decision as to whether the new born would live or die. *'Would the newborn's deformities still allow the infant to become a contributing member of the clan or ultimately a village burden?'*

If the infant's deformities were deemed to be a future burden on the village, the Head Man would immediately call for a Shadow Spirit Dance, to help assist the infant's shadow spirit on a safe journey passing over to the Spirit World. There the infant would have the opportunity to grow strong and healthy. The father would have the unpleasant task of smothering the infant sometime during the Shadow Spirit Dance.

This time the villagers didn't have long to wait. Some had just arrived when the Head Man emerged from the hut. From his grim and solemn appearance, everyone gathered knew the outcome, as the Head Man slowly shook his head from side to side. He was joined shortly afterward by a tall young man holding aloft his tiny offspring. This time the difficult decision would not have to be made, for the infant had been stillborn. To the amazement of all who saw the stillborn's body, she appeared to be perfectly formed, no deformities at all. Yet, she was too premature to allow any chance of drawing in the breath of life.

Traveler immediately recognized the young father as Blu, one of the men he had met at the water channels when he arrived. His heart ached as Blu held his stillborn infant aloft.

Many in the Rushing River Clan were apprehensive for Blu and his young mate, Kalu. The rumor being whispered in the wind among the Smokey Mountain Clan was that the couple was cursed. They had broken taboo and mated for love within the boundaries of their own clan. Although this was not formally banned, by custom, this was highly unusual. This had now been the couple's third stillborn birth out of four. Kalu was overwrought with grief and self-pity and had to be restrained for fear of her taking her own life with her black flake knife.

The Head Man immediately called for the Shadow Spirit Dance, lest another infant's shadow spirit wander the village in the dark; trapped between the present and the Spirit World. This would be troublesome for the cursed couple, since many of tehe village problems were already directed their way. The Smokey Mountain Clan were already convinced the wayward shadow spirit of the Kalu's last stillborn, was the cause of this year's worm infestation on the melon crop.

The frightened couple had tried to conceal the birth of their last child and the deformed infant had died after a three day struggle with life. Yet another three days passed before the grieving couple was caught trying to secretly bury the dead infant. The village had been thrown into an uproar, as tensions between the clans grew. The Head Man stepped in and ordered the infant's body to be seized for a belated Shadow Spirit Dance. Threats were directed at the young couple, since their selfishness of not willingly giving up the dead infant's body was depriving the village of baiting the ratta traps. Many claimed they had already felt the presence of the latest infant's wayward shadow spirit roaming about in the night.

The Smokey Mountain Clan had afterwards gathered and called for the formal banishment of Blu and Kalu, even knowing banishment would lead to certain death. They argued that customs cannot be set aside so easily or the whole village would suffer. But, that was not the sentiment of most of the Rushing River Clan. Many were friends or relatives of Blu and Kalu and pitied their losses. For them, banishment was out of the question. The villagers were beginning to choose sides and a deep rift was forming between the two clans. A violent clash between the clans was becoming more and more likely.

Bobane had finally stepped in and spoken out against any talk of banishment and the whispers had slowly quieted. Now, they were sure to start again after this new stillborn. Traveler overheard one of the Smokey Mountain Clan women ask another if she believed the two stillborn's shadow spirit's might now join forces to further torment the village.

Traveler felt bad for the young couple, for he, as his father before him, had faced unsavory rumors when their children had been born. *'He often wondered if his father had actually challenged the decision of his Head Man?'* After his mother died giving Traveler life, trading with the gods her life for his, his father had immediately taken him to live with his uncle in another village. Traveler's uncle had raised him for six rains before deeming the boy was strong enough to join his father on his journeys.

When Blu emerged from the hut carrying the tiny remains of his stillborn daughter, Traveler could easily see the young man's grief. But, the old man could also plainly see the man was frightened as well. It was especially obvious in his eyes, which darted here and there wearily at the gathered villagers.

Blu held his daughter's tiny remains high as he began the slow, solemn, shuffle and chant of the Shadow Spirit Dance. Most of the villagers reluctantly, slowly fell in line behind the grieving father as Blu shuffled around the clearing in a large circle. By custom, the infant's mother should have been behind her mate during the dance, but she was in little condition to do so. Those who took part, shuffled and chanted in the trance-like rhythm of the Shadow Spirit Dance, and with each revolution, the circle grew smaller and smaller. All the while Blu continued to hold his daughter's remains high as he chanted. After many revolutions of shuffling, the body of the dead infant slowly arrived at the village center, and the tightly wound circle of dancers halted. The grieving father, gently swaying from side to side as tears streamed down his face, held his daughter's remains even higher. The villagers joined him, swaying side to side, as they too raised their arms to the sky.

The Head Man, standing aside with his own arms spread, called out a final prayer.

"Earth Mother, we beseech you to grant this infant's shadow spirit a safe and peaceful passing. Entreat the gods, in their ultimate wisdom, to welcome her into the Spirit World, for she has no fault."

The villagers continued to stand and sway for a long time. Many in the group also implored the shadow spirit's journey be swift and uneventful. Others were just as certain, this would not be the case.

Once the Head Man finally lowered his hands, the villagers quickly dispersed to return to their daily chores. An elderly woman stepped forward to take the infant's earthly remains from the distraught father. He hesitated before solemnly placing the tiny remains of his stillborn daughter in the woman's hands. Taking a deep breath he wiped the tears from his face and turned back in the direction of his hut.

With the shadow spirit having passed over to the Spirit World, her empty remains would now be stored and allowed to rot. All the better bait for the tip-board traps. The ratta would come, the village would eat, and the circle of life would continue. That was the way.

chapter seven

"Mother's Warning"

As the villagers dispersed back to their huts or out to the fields, the village center returned to its normal routine. Traveler sat outside the Head Man's hut enjoying the early morning sun. He had just put on his eye-slits when people began approaching him. Waiting in turn, they greeted him politely and offered him a small item of food. Most of the food offered consisted of dried fruit or brown-nuts, but there were also slices of dried ratta and fresh melon. He thanked each villager in turn as he gratefully accepted their offerings. The old man knew this was the custom of The People regarding visitors, to welcome and share food, but he was overwhelmed by their generosity. Most of the offerings he dropped in his pack, only eating the fresh fruit or greens. When the greetings finally came to an end, and the old man raised his hand to the sun, he noted it had already risen two hands from the horizon.

Lowering his gaze, he was startled to see a young woman standing before him. He had not heard her approach, nor was she there to offer anything. She simply bowed her head and said, "Please come with me; you are expected."

The old man already knew who she was. She was Violeta, one of Mother's great-granddaughters. He stiffly rose from the log he was seated on with the help of his staff, and began to follow the young woman toward the edge of the village. He quickly realized Violeta was walking in the direction of Mother's tall, brown nut tree. As they approached, Traveler could easily make out Mother's large woven nests high above.

When they arrived at the base of the huge tree, Violeta motioned for him to stand in a particular spot and immediately turned back toward the village, not saying another word. Traveler momentarily turned to watch Violeta as she left, but the old man did not move from where he stood. He remained standing there for a few moments, expecting to hear a greeting from above. He was somewhat surprised when he heard nothing. *Surely, Mother knew he was there,* he thought. Traveler politely moved to within a few feet of the tree's trunk and called out, "Mother, may I visit, for I have need of your wisdom?"

Hearing no response, the old man turned to seek Violeta's assistance, but she had already vanished. He looked up and called out again. "Please, Mother, it is I, Traveler who seeks your wisdom. May I visit? It is your old friend Traveler."

Still, no reply came down from above. The old man was about to turn and go when he finally heard a young girl's voice call down from above. "I have heard many good things about you, Traveler. Yes, you may climb."

Traveler leaned his staff against the brown nut tree's trunk and looked for the easiest route to climb. Since the tree was secure within the boundary of the water channels, he noticed some small notches had been cut into the trunk to assist in climbing. Still, with his deformities and aching ankle, the old man struggled as he climbed. Upon reaching the lower nest of branches, Traveler was greeted by a young girl who offered her hand in help. Gratefully, he accepted her assistance as he made his way onto the interwoven branches of the lower nest. The branches were covered in woven grass mats.

"May I sit," the visitor politely asked the young girl? "This old man feels the fire in his knees from even the easiest of climbs."

"Of course," replied the girl. "Mother had told me to expect you, but I already knew you were coming as well. I have seen you in my nightly shadow visions, she did not need to tell me."

Traveler did not intend to be rude. Sitting and turning his full attention to the young girl, he was captivated by what he saw. His jaw dropped a little and his eyes opened wide as he stared. *'He knew it was possible, because he had already seen another; a boy far to the North. What he saw as he stared at the young girl was another perfect human!'* Like the boy he had seen, she appeared to have no deformities at all. Even her head was adorned with long, golden hair that flowed down loosely over her shoulders. She wore only a simple leather loin cloth. No cap, cape, or even an eye-slit marred her beauty.

The girl gave a little cough in her throat, to interrupt the visitor's rudeness. When Traveler overcame his shock, she turned her eyes upward to look at a second nest a little higher in the branches. She told the old man, "Mother lies in her sleeping nest above, but she has not been responsive to my voice in over a moon's cycle. I rejoice in the knowledge that her shadow spirit is very close to joining her relatives in the Spirit World. Especially Moa's spirit, with whom she was very close."

Traveler briefly glanced upward to where Mother lay in her nest before looking back again at the young girl. "You must be Emma," the old man stated before asking, "Where is your eye-slit?"

"Yes, I am Emma, and I have never worn an eye-slit. I cannot see in the dark like Mother and the others," Emma responded. "I am Mother's great-granddaughter. My mother's name was Jess, and my grandmother's name was Leta. They both cared for Mother before me. My mother, Jess, had nothing but good things to say about you."

"Yes, I knew Jess, but not as well as I knew your grandmother, Leta." Traveler responded before asking, "How is it that I have never seen you? I would have certainly remembered."

Emma replied, "Great-grandmother thought it best if I was safely kept in the trees, out of view and away from the villager's prying eyes and gossip. I was hiding from your view the last time you visited. I listened quietly to the words that were passed between you."

"You claim to have known I was coming? Are you a seer, too, like your great-grandmother?" Traveler asked.

"Yes, I guess you could call me a seer, but Mother referred to me more as a dream walker," she replied. "I see things in dreams, mine as well as others. I also have the ability to project my thoughts into other's dreams. That is why Mother has kept me hidden. She was afraid others would call me a witch."

"She was probably right."

"You said you knew my mother," Emma stated. "I bet you didn't know she couldn't see in the dark either. She only wore her eye-slit because she was afraid of what others might think."

Traveler paused to take in what the girl had just told him before asking, "How old are you, anyway?"

"With the coming rain I will be nine," she answered proudly.

The old man audibly sighed before taking in a deep breath.

"I know you think that is too young to be a seer, but Great-grandmother always knew I would carry the gift." The young girl added, "My mother told me that Great-grandmother even predicted my abilities before I was born. I do have visions; lots of them. Awake as well as in dreams. I just have difficultly finding their meaning. Great-grandmother has been helping me to better understand my visions."

Emma looked up toward the upper nest before continuing, "Great-grandmother told me once that my gift was much stronger than hers. She was helping me interpret one of my visions when she suddenly stopped responding. The last thing she said to me was 'Traveler will be here soon, your paths are intertwined. Go with him. They are waiting for you in the North.'"

Traveler asked, "Emma, may I see her? Maybe if I tried to speak with Mother she might respond. I sense her calling."

"Yes, I sense her too."

Emma led the old man over to the notched climbing pole leading up to where her great-grandmother lay, and Traveler awkwardly began to climb. The climb was much easier than the first. When he finally knelt down beside Mother's bed of leaves, the old woman noticeable stirred. Traveler gently reached over to take his old friend's wrinkled hand in his. At first Mother appeared to be asleep, and never once did she open her eyes, before she greeted him with a very soft, "Welcome, Traveler. We have been expecting you."

Emma rushed to her great-grandmother's side and gently lifted and cradled the old woman's head in her lap. Reaching for the nearby water skin she asked, "Great-grandmother, would you like some water?"

The old woman responded by opening her mouth a little, and Emma carefully poured in a few drops. "I'm so happy you have returned to me! You scared me so," Emma blurted out.

Mother softly replied, "Child, the time of my passing is growing near. Don't be sad or scared, for it is not a time of sorrow, but a time to rejoice. Emma, you must know this. I will never leave you. Even when I pass over, I will still be watching over you." The old woman paused to take a slow, deep breath. She seemed determined to say what she felt she must. "Now, you must go with Traveler. He is a wise man and will protect you. Use your gift to help him lead the clan to safety. You have shown him the vision and he knows the way."

Tears began rolling down the young girl's cheeks and she gently began to rock back and forth. Mother slowly opened her eyes and looked at the old man kneeling beside her. She again struggled to gather in a deep breath before slowly exhaling.

"Old Friend, we have been waiting for you, for I know you have seen Emma's shadow vision, too. You must take her with you and find the boy, for they are the future of The People. Take the clan north. The boy is waiting, for you are expected. The gift is strong with Emma, much stronger than mine." Mother struggled to take another slow, deep breath before adding, "Guard her well, and keep her beauty hidden. Especially from the Head Man, for he is pure evil. Violeta told me, Bobane killed Kia and Moa, but this I already knew. I'm sure Emma knows as well."

For a moment, all Traveler could think of was another long journey and was about to protest; to say his shadow spirit too, would soon pass over. But, before he could form the necessary words to utter his objection, Mother pulled her hand free from his and held it up, blocking his objections.

As if in answer to his unspoken protest, Mother softly said, "You are mistaken my dear friend. You still have many, many more rains on this side before your shadow spirit passes over."

The old woman struggled to take another deep breath before softly adding with her final words, "You must leave soon, the vision is growing stronger. The mountain is growing more angry with each passing day. You are the only one who knows the way. Take Emma! Take the clan! Find the boy and you find our future! This is your fate!"

With those final words, Mother's hand dropped to her side, and her shadow spirit began its passing. Seeing this, Emma's quiet sobs grew louder. Traveler moved over to take the young girl in his arms and draw her away from her great-grandmother's body. He held her for a long time before the poor child's sobs slowly began to ease. As he embraced the young girl, he gave thanks to Mother Earth and the gods for blessing Mother with such a long life.

The old man searched for other words that might console the grieving girl. "You may not see her, but your great-grandmother is still here. She just told you."

He gently tapped the young girl's chest and head with his fingers as he added, "She is here and here, and she will always be there. In your heart and mind. Your great-grandmother assured you herself, she will always be watching over you."

Traveler began to gather himself to stand, wishing to encourage Emma to leave her great-grandmother's remains. When Emma noticed the old man struggle so to stand up she quickly stood to help him. She saw him wince in pain as he tried to rise favoring his good leg. She gently pushed him back down to sit again.

Noticing the wrap on his ankle she asked "What is wrong with your ankle? And, I sense something is wrong with your head, as well? Maybe I can help."

Traveler explained his various ailments as best he could. He took off his hat and allowed Emma to look at the open sore on his head. After Emma had finished examining the old man's open wound, she faced him, nodding her head in confidence.

"Great-grandmother often spoke of a hot spring a short walk toward the setting sun," the young girl smiled as she spoke. "She told me the villagers won't go there because the water is sour and stinks like someone passing gas, but Mother said it has the power to heal. Soak in the yellow water and cover the sore on your head with the yellow, hot mud surrounding the spring. Do this for three mornings and I'm certain your ailments will begin to ease."

Traveler thanked Emma for her help and advice with a quick smile before placing his hand on her shoulder and stating, "I will definitely give your suggestion a try. I'll do it right now in fact. Afterwards, I must inform the Head Man of Mother's passing so the village can hold the Shadow Spirit Dance. I know your great grandmother's shadow spirit is eager to see her loved ones in the Spirit World. We should not keep them waiting too long."

Emma assisted Traveler back down the climbing pole to the lower level; the old man moving much slower than the nimble young girl. Once there, he turned to the grieving girl and said. "I have to leave you now. Say your goodbye's to your great-grandmother, but you must be quick. Then gather together your cap, shoulder cape, pack, and as much dried food as you have available."

Emma stood, looked back at him, her teary eyes opening wide as she shrugged her shoulders. "I have nothing of what you ask. I've never left the shelter of the tree, so there was never a need. Our food was brought each morning by Violeta. There is nothing here."

Traveler was taken aback with her answer. He thought for a short time before replying. "We're going to need help. I'll speak with some friends to see if they can assist us." He then took the young girl's hand in his. "I'm sorry, but I'm going to have to leave you for a while. Remember, you need to stay out of sight."

As he rose to leave he noticed Emma's bare feet. The old man added, "You're also going to need a covering for your feet, since they have not been travel-hardened."

"I'm sure my older sister Violeta, and her mate, Onyx, can help us," Emma quickly responds. "They live in the closest hut in the circle."

"Then that's where I'll go first," Traveler replied. "Maybe they can hide you in their hut. You heard Mother warn us that the Head Man should not see you. It would not be safe for you to be here in Mother's tree when they come for her remains." He reached over to pat her shoulder in reassurance. "Don't worry, everything will turn out fine."

Emma nodded her head in agreement, "I know," is all she said.

When Traveler left her at the brown nut tree, he couldn't help but think about her last response. *'Had she already seen her fate in a vision?'*

Traveler headed straight for Violeta's hut. He saw her sitting in the shade, with her back to the hut's wall. She was sewing on ratta leather with a bone awl.

"Ah, Traveler, did you get a chance to see Mother?" Violeta asked.

"Yes, I spoke with her. That's what brings me here," Traveler replied. "Your great-grandmother's shadow spirit has just passed over and is seeking entry to the Spirit World." He quickly added, "She asked me to take Emma with me when I leave."

"She said that to you? She actually spoke with you?" Violeta hesitantly asked the old man in disbelief.

"Yes, Emma was there too." He slowly nodded his head, momentarily deep in his own thoughts. As if talking to himself, he added, "Somehow she knew I have seen a boy, far to the North. A boy who, like Emma, has no deformities."

"What Mother sees never surprises me," Violeta replied matter-of-factly.

"She wishes for Emma and the boy to mate. By doing so, Mother seems to thinks it will somehow save The People." Traveler paused in thought before turning again to Violeta, "Mother did say something I didn't understand though. She said, 'They are waiting,' and, 'you are expected.' Do you have any idea what she might have meant by that?"

Violeta thought for a moment before slowly shaking her head side to side. "No," she answered.

"I already know the boy's village is located far to the North, but I don't understand how they could possibly be expecting us." Traveler paused in thought again before adding, "Mother also cautioned us to beware of Bobane. She felt something bad might happen if Emma is seen. She thinks the Head Man would try to force her to stay. Perhaps force her to be his mate."

Traveler took in a deep breath, "I have had the same thoughts. I don't know what it is, but something evil has spread amongst this village."

Violeta blurts out, "Yeah, the Smokey Mountain Clan and their head man. They're the evil. Bobane killed Kia. He hit him on the head with the stone club that hangs at his waist. Bobane thought nobody saw him do it, but Moa did."

"You suspect the Head Man might have killed Moa as well?" the old man blurted back surprised. "Mother just told me the same thing! She saw it in a shadow vision. Did you share your suspicions with Emma?"

"I started too, but she said she already knew. I didn't say anything else because I didn't want to upset her while she was dealing with Mother," Violeta replied. "She probably saw it in a dream. She does that a lot. The day before Moa died, he told me he confided what he saw to a friend. He was seeking his friend's advice on what to do. Whoever the friend was must have informed Bobane. That Head Man is pure evil as well as power hungry."

"All the more reason to leave as soon as possible," Traveler replied. "Mother was afraid of a shadow vision she had been having; one of a smoking volcano. The vision is a particularly strong one because Emma and I have both had the same vision; the same smoking mountain. I saw the mountain from the mountain pass. It's two or three mountain ranges to the South. Mother, and now Emma, insist we have to leave as soon as possible. The problem is, I need a large group of villagers to have any chance at success. Violeta, do you think you and Onyx would consider joining us?"

"I can only speak for myself, but, yes I would be very interested," Violeta replied. "I'm almost certain Onyx would too. He and Moa were very close, and Onyx has been talking about seeking some sort of revenge on Bobane. I've been trying to talk him out of it," she added. "I think he would welcome the chance to get away from the Smokey

Mountain Clan. I know a few others that might be willing to leave as well."

"Be very careful who you talk to," Traveler warned. "If Bobane learns of our plans beforehand there's no telling what he might do. Right now, when he learns about Mother's death I think he's definitely going to start searching for Emma."

The old man grew quiet, deep in thought. He then asked, "Emma mentioned a stinking hot spring, not too far from here. I have visited the village many times, but I've never heard of it. Do you how to get there?"

"Why would you want to go there?" Violeta asked. When the old man didn't respond, Violeta gave him the directions.

After listening to her directions, Traveler turned to go. Before he went far, he turned back to Violeta. "I need you to hide Emma in your hut. Make sure no one sees you bring her here. When I return from the hot springs, I'll inform Bobane of Mother's passing. Emma can't be at the tree when the clan elders go to fetch Mother's remains for the Shadow Spirit Dance. Emma understands this; she's expecting you."

"I'll go and fetch her right now then, and hide her here," Violeta responded. "Be careful when you speak with Bobane. He's two-faced. He acts pleasant to talk to, but behind that facade lies pure evil."

When Traveler left the hut, he headed directly to the hot springs. With the help of Violeta's directions, he found them easily. The hot springs gave off a horrid smell and stung his eyes as he approached. He reluctantly entered the smelly hot water and soaked, as Emma had instructed. He allowed the foul yellow water and stinking mud unhindered contact with his gashed ankle and the open sore on his head. Surprisingly, it didn't take long before he was completely relaxed lying in the hot mud and yellow water. The smell seemed to lesson the longer he stayed and he began to throughly enjoy the experience. He wondered to himself why he had never heard of the hot springs before. Maybe the smell was enough to discourage visitors.

When the old man had finished his soak his whole body felt rejuvenated. He vowed to himself he would continue the treatment in the coming days if he could.

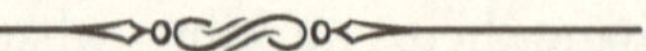

Returning to the village, Traveler made his way to the Head Man's hut. Finding nobody there, the old man assumed all the villagers were out working in the fields and he headed in that direction. It did not take him long before he located Bobane, working alongside three other men. They were busy digging out one of the water channels who's walls had collapsed inward, partially blocking the water flow. They were laughing and talking loudly amongst themselves as they worked.

Approaching the four men, Traveler quickly nodded his head, before sharing his solemn news. "I'm sorry to be the one to carry such sad tidings Bobane, but Mother's shadow spirit has passed this morning and is seeking entry to the Spirit World."

All the workers grew quiet as they heard the surprising news. They stopped digging, and set their tools aside. After a few moments, Bobane turned to the three men and directed them to inform all the field workers of the sad news.

"Does Violeta know?" Bobane asked.

"Yes, I have informed her," Traveler replied.

"Were you with Mother when her shadow spirit passed?" the Head Man inquired.

"Yes, I was sitting quietly holding her hand when her spirit emitted a long sigh and left her body. Mother never opened her eyes, nor did she utter any final words," Traveler lied. "Violeta told me she has not spoken to her in over a moon's cycle."

"Did you see the mystery girl, Emma?" Bobane inquired.

Again, Traveler lied. "No, I have never seen her, even in my past visits. I'm not so sure she even exists. If she did, why would Mother choose to hide her from me all these years? It doesn't make any sense."

As soon as word spread of Mother's shadow spirit passing, the Rushing River Clan women began preparing a feast befitting such a well respected clan member. The Smokey Mountain Clan had never even seen the old woman seer known as Mother, and they were baffled at all the fuss being made over an old women's passing. *'After all, she was just an old woman, living alone in a brown nut tree.'*

The Head Man gathered the Rushing River elders to retrieve Mother's body. Bobane respectfully walked a few steps behind the solemn procession as they made their way to Mother's brown nut tree. He was not there to help retrieve the old woman's remains though. He was there to search for Emma, the mystery girl he had heard so many rumors about.

The elders carefully lowered Mother's body to the ground, and carried her remains to Kia's hut. This was the custom for such an important member of the clan. Gathered at the hut were the old Head Man's women, patiently waiting to wash and prepare Mother's body for the Shadow Spirit Dance.

Bobane stayed behind at the brown nut tree as the elders left with the old woman's remains. He was determined to solve the mystery of Emma and slowly began to walk around the tree. His eyes searched every possible spot the mysterious girl could be hiding. When he had finished his search he walked back to the village frustrated; Emma was definitely not in the tree.

⸺◦◖◦◗◦⸺

The Shadow Spirit Dance began with the setting of the sun. The elders of the Rushing River Clan carried Mother's earthly remains aloft as they shuffled their feet and chanted the ritual prayers, employing the Gods to welcome Mother's shadow spirit into the Spirit World. Traveler shuffled along in the line of dancers in a place of honor, right behind the Elders. He was closely followed by Violeta and almost all of the Rushing River Clan. Emma peered out of the shadows of her sister Violeta's hut, as she mourned her great grandmother's passing all alone.

Only four members of the Smokey Mountain Clan chose to join the end of the slowly moving line. The rest stood respectfully, softly chanting on the sidelines. Bobane stood with them, his arms raised to the sky as he chanted, befitting a Head Man. As Traveler shuffled along to the rhythmic chanting he noticed Bobane openly glaring at the four members of his clan who had joined in the ceremony. The old man pondered Bobane's thoughts as he watched the Head Man continue to scowl at his four clansmen. Was their participation in the ceremony an act of defiance?

To the disappointment of the children, there would be no stories tonight. Following the Shadow Spirit Dance the feast honoring the well respected woman continued deep into the night. One after another, members of Mother's clan stepped forward to say something special about the seer.

Traveler had always considered Mother to be a dear friend, but he was somewhat astonished by hearing those who rose to speak. He had not realized the positive influence Mother had cast over the clan. No members of the Smokey Mountain Clan rose to speak. They did not know Mother.

When the villagers finally stood to return to their huts for the night, Bobane sought Traveler out. He quickly caught up to the old man as he was just about to enter Violeta and Onyx's hut.

"Traveler, may I have a word?"

The old man turned to face the Head Man. "I did not see Violeta's sister, Emma, at the ceremony," the Head Man stated. "If she were real I was certain she would be there. I was looking forward to finally meeting her." He paused a moment for Traveler to reply. When the old man did not offer a reply, Bobane shrugged before continuing. "Perhaps she is ill."

"I too, was looking forward to meeting her," Traveler lied discreetly.

"Perhaps she really is just a rumor, a whisper on the wind as you suggested. And, like most rumors, there is no truth behind them," Bobane said, carefully studying the old man's face before he continued, "Maybe she is resting here with her sister and we might be of assistance. What do you think?"

"I don't know, I haven't seen her, and I really haven't given it any thought," the old man cautiously replied. As he stepped toward the entrance, Traveler added, "The one thing I do know, is these old bones are exhausted, good night," and he turned, pushed the leather door flap aside, and ducked into the hut, letting the door flap fall behind him. Bobane was left standing outside.

Traveler stood quietly, just inside the darkened hut, listening.

His heart was beating rapidly, as he noticed Violeta, Onyx, and Emma standing nearby. They had obviously overheard everything. After a long pause, they were all relieved to finally hear the Head Man utter something under his breath and walk away.

"It's no longer safe for Emma to be here," Traveler stated quietly to the others. "Bobane is searching for her and I'm sure he will be back first thing in the morning. I think Mother's tree might be the safer spot now. He's already searched it and Emma has a hiding place there as well."

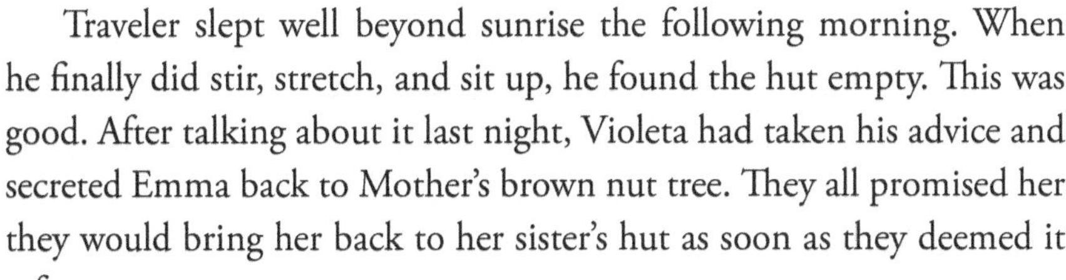

Traveler slept well beyond sunrise the following morning. When he finally did stir, stretch, and sit up, he found the hut empty. This was good. After talking about it last night, Violeta had taken his advice and secreted Emma back to Mother's brown nut tree. They all promised her they would bring her back to her sister's hut as soon as they deemed it safe.

The old man immediately left to visit the hot springs again to soak in the stinking yellow water. His ankle had stopped throbbing sometime the previous day. He had not actually realized it until he had finished the Spirit-Dance and was surprised when the pain was gone. The sore on his head felt different as well.

Returning to the village, after his visit to the hot springs, Traveler spent the rest of the day visiting old friends in their huts. For all those not needed in the fields, the interior of the mud huts, dug halfway into the cool earth, offered a blessed respite from the heat. Even the field workers spent a good portion of their time sheltering from the sun in the outlying field huts. Mid afternoon, during the hottest part of the day, most of the villagers took advantage of the huts' cool interiors to take a short nap.

During his visits with the villagers, Traveler began to spread a lie about a beautiful valley he had discovered, far to the North. He took no joy in lying to his friends, but in order for his plans to succeed he needed a large group of villagers to undertake the journey north with him. The old man was extremely confident he could always find a beautiful valley at the end of the journey, and in a way, that somewhat lessoned the remorse he was feeling for being untruthful. Traveler just didn't know exactly where that valley might be.

The old man continued by casually mentioning he was considering starting a new village there and asked if they might be interested in joining him. Quite a few said they would definitely consider it, if Traveler were able to persuade enough villagers to make the journey safe. Some even brought up their distaste for how Bobane and the Smokey Mountain Clan seemed to be taking over after the Rushing River Clan had generously offered them a new home.

One man took Traveler aside to quietly warn him, "Don't let Bobane learn of your plans. He's not the man he appears to be, and he'll stop at nothing if he thinks you are trying to take any villagers with you. He's ruthless and rules with that club that hangs at his side. I'm sure he murdered Kia, and wouldn't hesitate to do the same to you if he learns of your plans."

Traveler appreciated the man's frankness. "Thanks for your advice. I've heard this from others as well. Mother even told me the man was evil right before she passed. Tell the men joining us to come prepared with spears or clubs of their own. I don't want to fight Bobane, but we should be ready nevertheless. He might back down if we have a united show of force."

chapter eight

"Strange Creatures"

That evening after dinner the villagers once again gathered in the village center to hear more of Traveler's stories. The younger villagers were given the opportunity to sit around the log where the storyteller would eventually sit. They sat chattering excitedly with their friends until the old storyteller emerged from one of the nearby huts. The gathered children and villagers watched quietly in anticipation as Traveler stretched high his good arm, and then rubbed his extended belly in his way of showing thanks to the villagers for his evening meal. He then slowly walked over, and took his seat of honor on the central log. As he looked over the quiet gathering the old man rubbed his jaw as if he were deep in thought as to what story to begin with.

The gathering remained still and perfectly quiet as to not disturb the old man's thoughts. Finally, one of the young ones broke the silence by blurting out, "Please Traveler, tell us about the animals that came before."

This was exactly what the storyteller had hoped would happen, even though it was unusually rude for the boy to speak out before spoken to. He nodded his head and smiled at the young boy.

The storyteller smacked his lips and began. "In the time way back before the Great Change, many animals roamed the land; not just the ratta and soarers, but many others as well."

The storyteller stood up, and slowly climbed up to stand on the log. Raising his good arm high above, he bared his teeth and growled at the children seated below. They shuddered in anxious anticipation.

"One of those animals was a great white bar that lived in the far north. He was so big that even ten grown men of The People would not be able to lift him." Traveler sat back down before continuing. "The great white bar roamed a land where nothing would grow, not even a tree. He searched for water creatures to raise their heads out of the water to breathe. Then he would grab them in his teeth and jaws and devour them whole." As the old man said this, he jumped out at the children as if to catch them.

When the storyteller returned to his seat on the log, he nodded his head at the gathering, to assure the truth of the story. He then opened his eyes wide and looked from face to face before continuing. "He could even walk on water!"

One of the children shook his head and replied, "That could not be possible. If the white bar could walk on water, then the ratta could too, and the white bar would surely be eaten."

Another child asked, "If he is so big, how could the white bar walk on water without sinking?"

"Because, little one, the water in the far north gets so cold that it turns solid, like a rock." The old man reached down to pick up a rock. "Just as solid as this rock I hold in my hand."

"What do you mean when you say cold?" another asked. "I do not know that word."

Traveler thought a while before answering. "Where we live the days are always hot from the sun. In the far north where the great white bar lived, the sun was not so hot. In this land, where you could walk on water, the ancient human's had to wear many layers of hides over their bodies just to stay warm."

With many puzzled faces staring back at him, the old man added, "If you bring water in a clay jar back from the channel to your hut and leave the jar to sit all day in the sun, it will get hotter. Sometimes too hot to drink. If you leave the clay jar with water on the floor of your hut all day, it becomes cooler, and can be enjoyed. If you lived in the land of the great white bar, the water becomes so cool that it becomes solid."

Traveler continued, "Most of you have seen the red streams of lava flowing down the fiery mountains. The streams are very hot and they run swift like water. Pretty soon though, the red streams slow down as they cool and eventually stop, turning the lava solid like rocks. That is similar to what water does when it gets very cold."

Traveler knew these stories about water turning solid were not possible but he told the stories anyway, just as they had been told to him. He next told the children one of his favorites.

"There once was a creature with such long legs and such a long neck that it could eat leaves from the very top of the tallest trees. This creature was called a raff." Traveler held his hand high with his arm in front of his face in an attempt to show the animal's long neck.

Pointing to a tall tree near the village, he said, "See that tall tree? The raff's legs and neck were so long that it could reach leaves from the very top of that tree."

The storyteller looked at the children seated in front of him, nodding his head. They looked at one another and then up at the tall tree again. He continued, "The raff was one of Mother Earth's favorite animals so she gave the raff this great gift of a long neck so it would never go hungry. Food would always be within reach of the raff.

"Many animals would love to eat such a huge animal as the raff, but no other animal could jump high enough to grab the raft's neck. But, the Great Spirit made one big mistake. The raff was so tall that it could not easily reach the water below without taking a big risk."

Traveler stood and spread his legs as wide apart as he could and then used his arm stretched above his head to reach down and pretend his hand was reaching water. "Having to spread his front legs so wide apart just to allow the raff's head on top of such a long neck to get a drink of water, put the raff in great danger. The raff had to search the land thoroughly for possible enemies before even attempting to get a drink of water. Drinking was so dangerous for the raff, that they drank enough water at one time to last an entire day."

The storyteller asked the youngsters near him to stand and spread their feet as wide apart as they could so they could pretend to be a raff. Suddenly, Traveler yelled and jumped toward them. All of the pretend raffs were startled by the old man's actions and fell over backwards.

"All you little raffs are passing over to the Spirit World!" Traveler said as he helped a few children up before retaking his seat on the log.

"Now you know how dangerous it was for the raff to get a simple drink of water."

Traveler gave a yawn and reached for his walking staff.

"Please, Traveler, tell us one more animal story," one of the little girls pleaded.

The old man sighed and then slowly nodded. Holding up one finger Traveler said, "I will tell you one more. This story is about the strangest animal I have ever heard a storyteller speak of. This animal lived during the same time as the raff, and they were good friends.

"Close your eyes and see if you can picture this animal in your mind as I speak." Traveler paused while the children closed their eyes. "These giant beasts were bigger than the Head Man's hut, and so powerful that they could knock down a tall tree just to be able to feast on the tree's leaves and fruit." The storyteller noticed some of his listeners sat up a little straighter at his words. "They were called el-fants, and walked on four feet, each foot the size of your fire ring. El-fants had two giant teeth, as long as a grown man is tall, and yet they were gentle creatures like the raff, who only ate grass, leaves, and fruit."

"Their ears were bigger than the biggest shoulder cape. I know all that sounds very strange, but the strangest feature about an el-fant had to be their nose. An el-fant's nose hung all the way down to the ground, as long as three people are tall. The el-fants even drank water through their long nose. They could also use the end of their long nose as a hand to pick food up and put in their mouths."

"If you were brave enough, an el-fant would even allow you to ride on their back. Ten human's could easily ride on the back of one el-fant. Can you see the great el-fant in your mind?" Traveler asked as he stood. Removing his shoulder cape, he held the cape up to the side of his head with his withered hand. Bending over, the storyteller let his good arm hang down from his face as he walked a few steps, his arm swaying side to side.

The storyteller returned the same way, picking up his walking staff with his hand as he passed, and tucking it under his withered armpit. Some of the children stood to follow behind him into the dark, bending over at their waist with their arms swaying back and forth. With that, the evening's story telling was over.

Chapter Nine

"Making the Trade"

Traveler and Violeta had decided it was best if he sleep at the Head Man's hut that evening. They had come to the conclusion it might be easier to keep an eye and ear on Bobane until the time they departed. Everything was going according to plan, and they could meet during the day when Traveler made his normal visits amongst the villagers.

When the old storyteller ducked into the Head Man's hut, Bobane was already there. He sat quietly on the great hide and motioned Traveler to join him. Traveler took a seat on the hide across from the Head Man.

"Do you really believe the stories you tell?" Bobane asked Traveler? "Especially the one where you can walk on water?"

"Not really," the old man replied. "I just repeat what has been passed down for generations."

Bobane slowly nodded his head as he thought about Traveler's answer. "One thing I am curious to see, is the rock that look's back. Do you still have it?" Bobane asked.

"I have it here in my pack," Traveler responded. "I'd be happy to show you." He reached over to the nearby wall and dragged his pack over to him by its strap. Reaching into the pack, he pulled out what appeared to be a reddish rock, about the size of two fists clasped together. He handed the rock to Bobane. "It's better to look at the rock in the light of day. You may not see its mysteries and power as well in the dark."

Bobane took the rough, red rock the old man offered, and slowly turned it around in his hands as he examined it. He seemed surprised to find one side of the rock very smooth. He stared at the smooth side for a moment.

"You are looking into the very eye of the rock," the old man stated. "If you look carefully, and the light is just right, you will see your shadow spirit staring back at you. But, like I said before, the rock can show your shadow spirit better in the light."

Traveler continued, "I don't show the rock to people anymore because some I had shown, later accused me of being a sorcerer. They thought I used the power of the rock to capture their shadow spirit's. I really don't know how the rock's power works. I've seen my shadow spirit in the rock many times. I've even tried to talk to my shadow spirit, but he doesn't answer."

"Where did you find this rock?" Bobane asks.

"I found it, partially buried in the hard sand bank of a river, far to the West. The previous rainy moons must have exposed its hiding place. I was drawn to it out of curiosity when it reflected the sun's rays back at me. It took quite a bit of chipping to retrieve it from the sand-stone river bank."

"Do you think there may be others buried by the river?"

"I searched for the rest of the day, hoping that might be the case, but this is the only one I have ever seen." Traveler then added, casually studying the Head Man's face for a reaction, "I thought it might be something I could use in trade."

Traveler saw the Head Man's eyes slightly widen.

"I might be interested in trading for the rock, if you are still looking to trade," Bobane stated nonchalantly.

"I don't think so. I've become rather intrigued with it," the old man replied.

"Surely, there must be something you would accept in return?" Bobane said as he furtively looked around for something of value to offer Traveler. Unfortunately, he saw nothing to match the value Traveler would probably attach to the rock-that-looks-back.

"Ah, there is one thing I would consider trading the power of the rock for," the old storyteller said.

"And, what might that be?" Bobane replied, trying to think of something he possessed of equal value.

"I would consider trading for the animal hide we sit on," Traveler nonchalantly stated. "Perhaps you can convince your shadow spirit in the rock to talk to you."

"What could you do with that hide? You certainly can't carry it!"

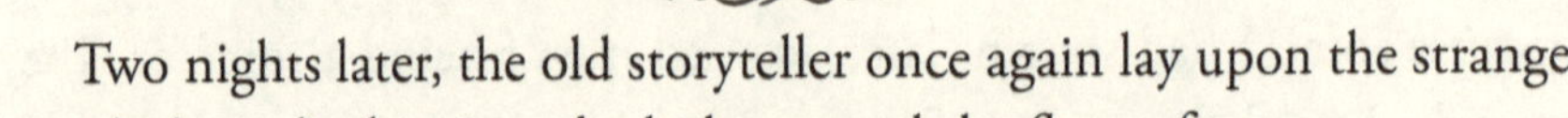

Two nights later, the old storyteller once again lay upon the strange huge hide, only this time the hide covered the floor of

Violeta and Onyx's hut. They had helped Traveler drag the hide from the Head Man's hut that afternoon. Although he was tired he had a hard time drifting off to sleep. He still couldn't believe Bobane had actually agreed to trade the hide for the rock-that-looks-back. Bobane had probably thought such an old man couldn't possible take the heavy hide with him and would have to leave it behind when he left. Then the Head Man would simply return it to its proper place. Only, Traveler had another idea about how to best use the great hide that might come in handy for his group during their upcoming journey.

chapter ten

"Shadow Visions"

Traveler finally dropped off into a troubled sleep. Something began to torment his sleep almost immediately and he began to toss and turn. The night shadow vision's finally forced their way into Traveler's dreams. The first shadow vision that appeared took the form of an old man, slowly materializing from the edges of his consciousness. The vision was standing on the slope of a fiery volcano, looking up. The shadow vision watched as the lava freely flowed down the slope toward him. However, the flowing lava was quickly overtaken by a thick cloud of gases rushing down from the volcano's peak. Resigned to his fate, and without muttering a word, the shadow vision watched as the toxic cloud of gases rolled over him, swallowing him up in its downward rush. Traveler's mind tried to draw the spirit back, but to no avail.

As morning approached, a second shadow vision appeared in the old man's dreams. This time the shadow vision slowly took the shape of a beautiful young woman, standing on a river bank. She was gazing over an empty, muddy river bed. What little water remained in the river bed was confined to puddles. Traveler saw giant fish flopping about on the river's muddy bed as giant river terrors slowly moved from fish to fish on stubby legs, devouring each in turn.

The old man awoke with a jerk shortly after the young women of the shadow vision in his dreams hurried down the steep river bank and out onto the muddy river's bed. Suddenly she turned back, beckoning him to follow before slowly fading from his mind. Somehow the vision seemed familiar… ?

Traveler is certain the two shadow visions were trying to warn him and he lay awake trying to understand the meaning of his visions. He had shared his previous night's shadow visions with the Head Man and some elders before Mother's Shadow Spirit Dance, and he once again felt compelled to do so.

He waited until first light appeared in the hut's smoke hole, quietly rose, and ducked out of the hut. The old man quickly made his way to the Head Man's hut where he politely greeted a woman busy cooking the morning porridge outside the hut's entrance. He pushed the door flap aside and ducted in.

Traveler sat patiently on the woven mat covering the earthen bench and waited for the others in the hut to stir. A short time later, he watched as the woman pushed aside the leather door flap with her shoulder and ducked into the hut carrying the clay pot containing the morning's porridge. She set the steaming porridge on the floor and ducked back outside. Those inside slowly began to stir and gather around the clay pot to eat. Traveler joined the others as they began to dip their fingers into the pot and scoop out the warm porridge.

Traveler didn't eat much before he began to lick his fingers clean and back away from the pot. He took a seat back on the mat covered bench and waited for the others to finish their morning meal. When the pot was finally wiped clean the men began to politely lick their fingers. Traveler couldn't contain himself any longer and blurted out, "Last night I had two more shadow vision's visit my dreams. Just like the night before, I think they're trying to warn us."

The elders looked to Bobane to speak, not wanting to be rude.

"I didn't know you stayed with us last night, Traveler," Bobane said.

"I did not. I came early to tell you of my visions," Traveler responded.

Bobane nodded in understanding. "Then tell us of these new shadow visions," the Head Man responded.

After telling Bobane and the elders about his recent shadow visions, Traveler asked, "What do you think they mean?" He looked around the hut, quietly waiting for an answer.

The elders again deferred to the Head Man to respond and after much thought, Bobane finally replied, "I have thought a great deal about yesterday's shadow vision; the one with the smoking mountain. It might refer to a volcano some of us have seen, far to the South. We passed it when we journeyed from our previous village much farther south. We named the mountain, The Sleeping Giant, because it was constantly making soft rumbles like someone snoring."

"Why would the shadow vision tell me to go there? I have no knowledge of this mountain," Traveler responded. He thought about it a few moments before adding, "I'm sure all the visions are somehow connected."

"I don't know the answer to that. How can a smoking volcano and an empty river be connected?" One of the elders asked, before adding his opinion. "Maybe these visions were just bad dreams. We all have bad dreams from time to time."

"I have never had shadow visions disturb my sleep like this before," Traveler replied matter of factly. "And, they only recently started. I think you hear me, but you do not listen. To me the shadow visions seem to be a warning. I think they want me to move away from that smoking mountain, not toward it."

Traveler suddenly thought, why not use the visions to help with his plans. After a few moments, he nodded his head and smacked his lips in deep thought. "I have decided to listen to these warnings. I will leave here in four days and head east. I believe that's the direction the shadow vision pointed. I do not know the meaning of the empty river vision, but I believe that too, will become clear at some point."

Traveler was rapidly working out in his mind how his visions would help his plan actually work. There was no question in his mind as to what direction he planned to travel, and it certainly wasn't east. Mother had told him clearly to head north. Plus, that is the direction of the boy's village. He certainly didn't trust Bobane or the Smokey Mountain

Clan elders enough to share this detail of his plan. He would first head east and then turn north once he was sure he was not being followed by one of Bobane's spies.

chapter eleven

"Scar"

The storyteller wanted to stay on good terms with Bobane, and he quickly changed the subject. He faced the Head Man and stated, "You asked me about Scar, when I first greeted you. I don't often talk about my companion but I will share with you and the elders how I was able to befriend such a strange creature. That is, if you are still interested."

"Scar is the name of the creature that used to travel with you?" Bobane asked.

"The name seemed appropriate," Traveler replied. "When you hear her story you will better understand her name."

"I think the elders would very much like to hear your story, as would I," Bobane responded.

Traveler thought back to the very first time he had laid eyes on Scar. He took a slow, deep breath and began.

"I had just finished guiding three young men between two northern villages and was not expected at the Little Lake village for over a moon. I suddenly had an urge to see another animal similar to the one I had once seen guiding with my father as a young boy. A creature so hideous looking, with bones growing out the top of its head, that I felt pity for the beast's deformity. My father had surprised me later when he suggested the bones might not have been a deformity at all. Unfortunately we didn't have a chance to get closer before the creature quickly vanished into the shadows of the forest."

"Neither my father nor I had ever encountered such a large creature before and since I knew I was just a few days walk south of the area we had first seen it, I decided to head north in hopes of seeing another. Maybe I could solve the mystery of the bones once and for all."

Traveler continued, "The search did not go as I envisioned and I became lost for days. Luckily, the gods favored me, and I stumbled upon an unknown village far to the North. When I approached the village I was surprised to see the villagers wearing long, soft, leather shirts, as well as sandals."

"Why would they be so foolish to wear such hides in such heat?" one of the elders asked.

"They said the weather was not always hot in the forest they lived in, and the tops offered easy protection from the little biting insects they had in swarms," Traveler replied. "We rub mud on our bodies to protect us. Plus, the animal skins they wear are much softer and pliable than any of the dried ratta skins we use."

"Anyway," Traveler continued, "the villagers welcomed me warmly and quickly confirmed the existence of the creature I sought. They told me I might see many hands of them if I traveled north-east. They told me their shirts were made from the very animals I sought. The Head Man showed me one of the hides the village women were working on at the time. One of the women explained the process used to soften the hides for use. We should try it on our ratta hides, but that is a story for another time."

"The villagers were right. After just a day of walking, I found numerous tracks in the mud around a small stream. For some reason I felt certain the tracks were from the creature I sought; the animal my father and I had observed so many rains before. A short time later, I found what I had been searching for. Only the great creature was dead. It was obvious from its surroundings that it had fought valiantly before falling victim in a great battle. Two other large, unknown animals lay dead near the bony headed creature I sought."

Those in the Head Man's hut sat spellbound as Traveler continued his story. All who listened sat quietly, as nobody wished to interrupt the story teller's train of thought.

"When I cautiously approached to examine the three strange beasts lying on the forest floor," Traveler continued, "I was surprised to find one of the strange animals was not dead at all. She lay quietly on her side, too weak to move, but still alive. Her breathing was slow and shallow, but her eyes remained alert as she watched my approach. A long, open gash ran halfway down her side, beginning at her shoulder. I had never seen such an animal before but it was readily apparent she had been gored by one of the bloody bones that protruded from her adversary's head. From the red gore of the grass she lay on, it was obvious she had already lost a great deal of blood. She struggled weakly to raise her head as I bent down to examine her wound, but was unable to do so. She then closed her eyes and eased her head back down, accepting her fate."

"My first thought was to bash the wounded beast's head in with the heavy end of my walking staff and send her to the Spirit-World; or wherever such beasts go. In fact, it would have been the merciful course of action. I was raising my staff to do just that when the animal opened her eyes again to look at me. I heard a soft whine emitting from her throat and she attempted once again to raise her head."

"I have often thought later about that very moment. I still remember the feeling that I had at the time. I held her life or death in my hands and the creature was requesting a chance to live. After a few moments she once again relaxed her head, closed her eyes, and awaited my decision."

"I'm still unable to explain my decision that day, but I lowered my walking staff, and reached for my pack. That turned out to be one of the best decisions of my life. I gave her water from my water bag by gently dripping it into her mouth. Her fierce teeth, just a hand's length away, offered no threat. It may sound strange, but even though she was too weak to resist, I somehow felt her gratitude."

"Digging around in my pack, I found the ingredients I needed to make a simple herb poultice and applied it to her wound in an attempt to stop her bleeding. The very same poultice I would apply to my own wounds, if I were injured."

"I had just finished applying the poultice when I heard growling sounds rapidly approaching through the forest. I remember being terrified, dropping everything and scrambling up the nearest tree. I gained a precarious hold just in the nick of time, too. Unfortunately, the nearest tree was also the smallest and weakest tree and it slowly began to bend over."

"Five beasts, similar to the one I was aiding, sprang into the clearing, returning to feast on the huge boney animal's remains. Two of the animals immediately saw me clinging to the thin tree trunk and attacked. They let out terrifying growls and leapt as high as they could in a futile attempt to dislodge me from my perch. Their jaws were snapping just fingers away. Of course, this brought the attention of the whole pack, and they all went into a frenzy as they too attempted to reach me with their teeth. I thought for sure I was doomed, but somehow, I was able to extend my walking staff out and lodge the head between the branches of a nearby tree. Holding on tightly with one arm I was able to stop my tree's slow bend."

Traveler smiled to himself as he talked, thinking how comical he must have looked. He had seldom told this story before, but he never failed in having a good laugh at his predicament.

Traveler let out a small chuckle before resuming. "When the beasts finally realized I was just out of reach they turned their attention back to the kill they had previously made. I watched in fascination as the beasts tore huge chunks from the carcass, swallowing the meat in large gulps. It was only when they had consumed their fill, that one of the pack standing close to the wounded animal took notice when the injured member of the pack raised her head and whined. The two nearest animals rushed over to their wounded companion and began to lick her snout and ears, obviously encouraging her to stand. Other members of the pack trotted over to do the same. I watched as one by one they all sniffed the poultice I had applied to her wound, but luckily none of them disturbed it."

"They all seemed to sense the danger their wounded companion would be in if they left, so they settled down for the night, laying all around her. All the while I was struggling to prop myself up with my staff, holding on with one arm."

"The wild pack left at first light, leaving the injured animal behind. I literally fell out of the tree since I was unable to use my cramped arm. I gave thanks to Mother Earth that the wild pack had left my backpack untouched. For unknown reasons, I felt the need to continue treating the wounded creature. I knew she must be thirsty so I quickly gave her another long drink of water. I could easily see her eyes were much more alert as she watched my every move. I gently lifted her head and slowly poured in the water. She was still too weak to resist my touch but readily drank the water I offered."

"I softly talked to her as I treated her; a habit I continued to do throughout our long relationship. I sat beside her, giving her water all through the day, along with slices of meat I cut from the boney-headed beast. As I dropped them into the her mouth, I remember saying, 'One for you, one for me.'"

"I examined the beast's torn side and was pleased to see that the poultice had stanched her bleeding. I left the poultice in place, afraid that changing it might reopen the wound. I was ready when her pack returned again that evening, aloft in one of the larger trees when they trotted back in at dusk. I watched as they went straight to their wounded pack mate, each licking the wounded animal's snout. They seemed very excited, whining and barking, sensing that she was recovering."

"The same pattern continued for the next two days. I watched as the pack fed on the carcass at dusk, and was surprised to see each member of the pack bring the wounded animal small pieces of meat. Each evening, after the pack had eaten their fill, they settled down next to their wounded pack mate, guarding her throughout the night from any marauding ratta that might venture too close. I'm certain the pack all knew I was up in the tree watching them, but they totally ignored me after the first night."

"On the fourth day, the injured animal allowed me to change the poultice on her side. We seemed to have developed a mutual sense of trust in one another. The creature seemed to understand that I was helping her. I continued to sit by her side all day, as I had over the previous two days, offering her small strips of meat and water. All the while I softly talked to her."

"Then it happened. To my great surprise, she abruptly stood up. I remember scrambling back in shock and fear; stumbling, and falling into a sitting position. I was so scared all I could do was sit there, as she slowly limped over and stood over me. She was a hand away and I felt her warm breath on my face. She did not growl, or even show her teeth, but instead straddled me and looked deep into my eyes. Her shoulders stood taller than my head and I knew I dare not move. After what seemed like an eternity, the fierce animal simply turned, limped back to her previous spot, and lay back down."

"Later, when I think back to that moment, I feel certain she was making a decision; a life or death decision. Similar to the one I had made previously with her. I had been so frightened, followed by such relief, that it took a long time to regain my feet and climb back up to the safety of the tree. She watched me the entire time, but she did not move. It was sometime during that night, she left with her pack. Their big kill had been completely consumed."

"I remember having all sorts of emotions when I woke and she was gone; relief, sadness, but most importantly, proud of my accomplishments. Thankful of the opportunity to help one of Mother Earth's creatures. I remember saying a prayer of thanks to the gods for the blessings they bestowed upon me. Besides saving the life of an unknown creature, I had located an isolated village, and found the bony headed animal I had set out to find."

Traveler thought to himself, as he let his words be absorbed by the men in the hut, *'and met an incredible young man.'* There was no way Traveler could know the role that young man would play in his not too distant future.

"That's quite a story, but you haven't said how Scar ended up as your companion," Bobane stated.

"My best answer to that," Traveler replied, "is I don't know. I don't know how Scar found me, or continued to find me."

"It was a number of moons later that we were reunited, far to the South. I had recently finished guiding three young men from one village to another and I didn't want to overstay my welcome. I had been the clan's guest for over a moon's cycle, and it was time to move on. Since I had no young men to guide, I decided to visit my old friend, Mother. I needed to reach the river crossing before the rainy moons made the crossing impassable."

"I had been on the journey to Mother's for a handful of days and was busy cooking my supper when I saw a large animal trotting towards me. I had never seen such an animal in the areas I travel and I immediately climbed up the brown nut tree I was under. I instantly recognized the type of animal from my encounter with Scar's pack only a few moon's back. I was both terrified and excited."

"I was even more dumbfounded when the animal simply trotted over and lay down at the base of the tree I was in. My fear quickly turned to excitement. I just couldn't believe it! I could easily see the animal was definitely a female, but could this possibly be the same animal I had nursed back to health? At the moment I couldn't be sure, but my excitement was growing. I remember beginning to talk softly to her, trying to get her to turn her body around so I could see her other flank. The one that would have been scarred."

"But, she just lay still, intently listening to the words I spoke to her from above. I could see her eyes studying my every move but I dare not descend until I was certain. She finally rose, turned and jogged off into the falling gloom. It was only then that I could easily see the long, ragged scar that ran along her side. I remembered the feeling of excitement wash over me. It was indeed the same animal, of that I was now certain. A handful of questions I could not answer then came to mind. *Why did she come to visit me? Did I lose my opportunity to befriend her by remaining in the tree? Stranger yet, how did she find me?'* That last question remains a mystery to this day."

"The next morning Scar returned at first light carrying a fat ratta. She jogged right up to my tree and dropped the dead ratta at the base of the tree's trunk. She then backed off a short ways away and lay down. Her eyes continued to move between me and the dead rata. She was obviously saying, *'My move.'*"

"Then I thought, *'could she be trying to bait me to come down from the safety of the tree?'* I watched and talked to her for a long time before I cautiously decided to take a chance and descend from the tree. I didn't have much confidence in defending myself against such a ferocious animal, but I held my walking staff ready to swing any way. Scar did not move, but continued to watch as I descended to the ground."

"I cut the fat ratta with my black flake knife into small strips, tossing pieces to her as I shared her offering. I definitely prefer my meat cooked, but I didn't want to wait, for fear the creature might become agitated at the delay. Plus, I had no idea how she would react to a fire. It was that very day I named her Scar. We have been odd companions ever since."

"I've been told that Scar will not come into the village, but remains outside the outer channels," Bobane said. "Why is that?"

"I think that's just a matter of trust. Right now she trusts only me. Humans have undoubtedly hunted her pack in the past, so her trust does not extend to others. When we approach a village, she refuses to enter. Instead, she'll remain at the outer fringes of the village, sometimes even in plain view. Even when I stay for a moon or more, Scar will continue to wait patiently for me, rejoining me only when I begin to wander again on a new journey."

"If I'm accompanied by young men, which is generally the case, Scar is very protective of me. She insists everyone keeps a cautious distance from me. She'll quickly let them know with a growl if they venture too near. Fortunately, she has never had to do anything more. I always inform anyone traveling with me to keep their distance and everything will be OK. So far we haven't had a problem."

Traveler continues, "When I journey, Scar follows a simple routine. She walks at my side during the day while I talk to her for hours on end, mostly repeating The People's stories out loud to maintain my memory. At the end of the each day, Scar disappears into the darkness to hunt, but she always waits until I've safely ascended to my night's nest before trotting off. She usually returns at first light, and seldom without a fat ratta to drop at the base of my tree."

"Unfortunately," Traveler concluded, "it seems Scar is gone for good this time, but I'll forever be grateful to Mother Earth for the time she allowed me to share with one of her magnificent creatures."

With that, the old man stood and ducked out the door of Bovane's hut.

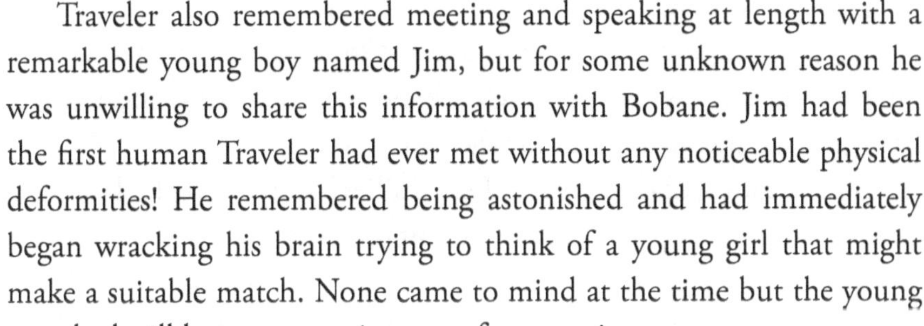

Traveler also remembered meeting and speaking at length with a remarkable young boy named Jim, but for some unknown reason he was unwilling to share this information with Bobane. Jim had been the first human Traveler had ever met without any noticeable physical deformities! He remembered being astonished and had immediately began wracking his brain trying to think of a young girl that might make a suitable match. None came to mind at the time but the young man had still been many rains away from mating age.

Somehow, Mother had learned of the young man who lived far to the North and asked Traveler to take Emma to him. The old man was only now beginning to realize the significance this match might have on The People's future. The perfect match.

chapter twelve

"Planning to Leave"

When Traveler left Bobane's hut, he headed straight back to Violeta and Onyx's. He scratched at the door frame and was invited in. Violeta and Onyx, greeted him when he entered. Violeta was excited to tell the old man her news, and blurted out, "Onyx wants to go with us when we leave."

"I've already gathered three other families," Onyx added. "It will be good to break free of the Smokey Mountain Clan."

"Keep this information to ourselves. Right now Bobane thinks I will be leaving alone. And Onyx, remember, I have invited some members of the Smokey Mountain Clan to go with us, so watch what you say," Traveler cautioned. "We will be forming a new clan; all of us together. A clan devoid of hate and deceit."

"Don't worry about me, Traveler. I understand what you're saying. I have some good friends in the Smokey Mountain Clan. By the way, what do you plan to do with this hide we dragged over here yesterday?" Onyx asked, looking down at the hide he stood on. "Did we steal it from Bobane?"

"That's want I wanted to speak with you about."

Traveler then told the young couple about his trade with the Head Man, and explained to them in detail exactly what he planned to do with the hide.

"It's a shame to have to do that, but it's probably for the best," Onyx replied. "It would be hard to carry it the way it is now. I'll gather the men who have agreed to go with us, and get to work on it right away. It shouldn't take too long."

Traveler nodded his approval, and Onyx ducked out of the hut. The old man then turned to Violeta to ask, "How's Emma doing?"

"She's broken hearted, but doing as well as can be expected. Better than most who've lost someone as close as Mother."

"Listen. Once again, I'm certain Bobane will find some excuse for a surprise visit to your hut this morning. He hinted so at the morning meal. Emma should go back to Mother's tree for the day."

"OK, if that's what you think," Violeta nodded. "After Bobane comes by, then I'll sneak Emma back. She shouldn't be alone at this time. I give you my word, Traveler, Bobane will not find her."

"I hope not. That would surely mean trouble," the old man replied. "I'll see you tonight. I have to go and let the people know we leave in four days."

Traveler turned and ducked out the door, looking forward to visiting the hot springs. Emma's mud treatment was working miracles on his various ailments. His whole body felt stronger and more energized, and he enjoyed relaxing in the warm mud. He also could take this opportunity to formulate the details of his plan in his mind.

Talk of the storyteller 's shadow visions, and his sudden decision to leave, spread quickly throughout the village. Traveler was well respected amongst the Rushing River Clan and they all knew he originally planned to stay in the village for at least another moon, leaving with the coming of the rains. Once the rains started, the ratta would withdraw into their dens, and traveling would be safer; albeit a little less comfortable. The old man certainly would not change his plans so suddenly unless he really took his shadow visions seriously.

Traveler had just emerged from visiting another friend's hut, when he was approached by the young father, Blu, whose woman had had the unfortunate stillborn birthing. Blu was a good head taller than the storyteller as he rushed over to stand in front of Traveler, blocking the old man's way.

"Take us with you!" Blu blurted out pleadingly.

"I wander alone," Traveler cautiously replied. He then inquired, "Why do you want to go with me, you hardly know me and even I don't know where my trail leads?"

"Wherever it may lead, it leads away from here," replied the man sarcastically. "Kalu is terrified. Some friends have told her about the whispers in the wind spreading around foretelling of our coming banishment. This time they say the talk is growing more persistent. They have even heard that Bobane has agreed. If the Head Man banishes us, we will die."

"I'm sorry, I only carry enough food for myself. I do not have enough to share," Traveler responded.

"We have food. Dried fruit, nuts, and lots of smoked ratta," the man replied. "If you take us with you we will gladly share. My family will carry everything, including your pack. And, my women can do your cooking. They are all very good cooks. I beg of you, please take us with you."

Traveler heard the desperation in the man's voice and saw the fear on his face. "Maybe that might work," the old man nodded, smiling inwardly to himself, "but, this must remain only between ourselves, our secret."

Blu grabbed Traveler's good hand with both of his and squeezed, "Thank you, thank you! You won't regret it, you'll see, we can be of great help to you."

Traveler's hand hurt in the young man's grip and he tried unsuccessfully to pull away. "You can first help by giving my hand back," the old man winced as he nodded toward his hand.

"Sorry, sorry, please forgive me," the young man apologized profusely, bowing more than once.

"You need to know something before we leave," Traveler warned, "I am old, and my spirit is tired and may choose to pass over to the Spirit

World any day. What will you and Kalu do if my spirit reaches this decision while we travel?"

"That is a risk my women and I most willingly will take," the man replied excitedly before running off to tell his family to pack.

"Wait!" Traveler called after him.

Blu immediately returned and stood apprehensively in front of the old man.

"Bring a couple of spears with you, just in case there is trouble."

"I don't have any," the young man said.

"Well then, make some," Traveler replied, a little annoyed.

Traveler watched as Blu turned and jogged away. He envied the strength of youth in the man's jog. *'Maybe this will be a good thing,'* he thought to himself. *'Blu may not know it, but he appears to be a born warrior.'*

The next day, three more individuals and two other family groups cautiously approached the storyteller asking if they might join him on his journey. When Traveler asked why they desired to take on such a hard and dangerous journey, they gave a variety of reasons. Some were friends of the first young couple and just wanted to go where they went. Another young man wanted to see more of the land around him, intrigued by Traveler's descriptions of his travels. Two women, who lived in the same hut, wanted to get away from their mutual mate; a man who beat them. They promised to assist Traveler and care for his needs. And, one young couple simply told the old man, they hoped he would be heading north so they could see for themselves the land where one could walk on hard water.

Traveler cautioned them all to keep this journey their secret, not to mention anything to members of the Smokey Mountain Clan. And, all the men were asked to carry spears or clubs for protection.

The old man knew that those planning on leaving would not be able to keep their secret from their friends. Although Traveler had cautioned each group about keeping their plans to themselves, he knew this was unlikely. He was actually hoping they would share their secret with their close friends. His main concern was still the Head Man, but so far, neither Bobane, nor members of the Smokey Mountain Clan appeared suspicious of their journey. They were all aware he was leaving, they just didn't know others were now planning to leave as well. As far as they knew, Traveler was just visiting friends to say goodbye.

Throughout the day, more and more people approached Traveler, quietly asking to join the exodus. Each time, he agreed to guide them and explained to them what supplies they would need. The group would leave at daybreak on the fourth sun's rising.

Traveler planned to sleep the following three nights in different friend's huts. He was concerned Bobane might learn of his plan if he slept another night at the Head Man's hut. Bobane was always asking him questions and might catch him in a lie. He also thought it might put Emma in danger by drawing Bobane to Violeta and Onyx's hut, if he stayed there again. Anyway, changing sleeping spots was not unusual for a storyteller when he visited villages. People were always inviting him to join them for supper and stay the night for they were eager to hear news of their loved ones living in other clans. A few, after sharing a meal with him, took the opportunity to ask the old man about his leaving. They had heard whispers in the wind and wanted to know more about his upcoming journey. *'Where was this beautiful valley he spoke so fondly of? Did it have good water? Was the ground fertile? How many day's journey would it involve?'*

chapter thirteen

"Disaster"

Two mornings before Traveler planned to leave, tragedy struck the village. He had just returned from a sunrise soak in the hot springs and was standing outside Jo and Luke's hut. He had spent the previous night there and had just finished a late breakfast of porridge and melon. The old man was talking to a small group of men about the upcoming journey, when they heard a girl suddenly start screaming. The screams were coming from Violeta and Onyx's hut, and the old man instantly knew it was Emma.

"Get out of the hut! Get out! Get out right now!" the girl franticly screamed. "Hurry! Hurry!"

When Traveler turned toward his friend's nearby hut, where the commotion emanated from, he saw Violeta, Onyx, and four little kids run from their hut. Emma emerged moments later, and began to run about the nearby huts shouting her warning to any villagers who would listen, "Get out of your huts! Get out of your huts!"

Fortunately, most of the villagers had already left to work in the fields, but most of those still left in the nearby huts, mainly women and children, quickly stepped out to see what all the yelling was about. What they saw and heard were the shouts of a strange young girl, with long golden hair, running about the village center, screaming for everybody to get out of their huts. They watched, in total confusion, as the strange girl continued to run about urgently crying out her warning. "Get out of your huts!"

Suddenly, the sound of loud, distant, explosions reverberated throughout the village. Everyone instantly turned their attention from the mysterious girl and looked to the South, the direction of the sound's origin. Within moments of the first loud explosions, Mother Earth began to wreak havoc on the land of The People. An invisible force suddenly jerked to the side the very ground the villagers stood upon. Unlike the almost daily tremors of the past, the movement of this jolt was far more violent and intense.

Traveler's small group, along with everyone else within the village center, were violently jerked off their feet and slammed to the undulating ground. Terrified villagers screamed, desperately clinging to whatever they could reach, and held on tight. However, most were unable to grab hold of anything, being in the village center, and were tossed about in terror as the ground's surface continued to roll like huge ripples on water.

As the undulating ground tossed the frightened villagers helplessly about, a deafening noise arose throughout the village as the earth's crust suddenly ripped apart. Starting at the river's edge, a huge fissure tore its way through the village center and disappeared over the distant ridge beyond, leaving hundreds of uprooted and splintered trees in its path.

The prolonged guttural moaning reverberating from the ruptured earth, along with the crashing of trees and huts, was unlike anything the old man had ever heard or experienced. Even with the ongoing terror of the earth's surface undulating beneath him, Traveler's eyes followed the rip as it tore asunder the earth's crust before vanishing up and over the ridge high above the village. The huge dust cloud the fissure generated, along with the drama of splintering trees falling in the fissure's path, was mesmerizing to Traveler as he watched.

With the ground continuing to heave and roll, the old man wondered if his shadow spirit would pick this moment to pass over. Maybe Mother had been wrong in her prediction for his life.

Finally, Mother Earth grew exhausted from her erratic shaking and fell into a fitful slumber. With the shaking stopped, the terrible moaning coming from within the deep crack also eased. Even with a few continuing screams of pain, compared to what transpired just moments before, silence seemed to prevail around the old man.

Traveler lay on the ground for some time before his mind finally heard the very weak screams for help. The old man, surprised to still be in the Real World, was hesitant to stand as he turned to look for the scream's source. He replaced his dislodged eye-slits, and his eyes widened as he peered through the narrow slits in disbelief. Where, just a few moments ago, there had stood a vast ring of huts, half had now vanished, swallowed up by the massive crack. The desperate screams for help were coming from down in the crack itself!

Traveler quickly glanced around a moment in search of his walking staff. Not immediately seeing it, he rose to his knees and stood up with some difficulty. Most of the people around him were already making their way to, or standing, at the crack's edge, looking down. The old man finally located and retrieved his walking staff a short distance away before cautiously approaching the crack's edge.

The ground on the far side of the crack had completely collapsed three of four times a grown man's height. A few of the damaged huts were precariously perched on a collapsed narrow section of ground clinging to the fissure's far side. A few survivors and injured were gathered amongst these huts, frantically calling out for help from those above. All the other missing huts had fallen into the depths below, vanished from sight.

Traveler peered down into the fissure's depths in search of the missing huts, but he saw nothing. He couldn't even see the bottom of the fissure. He yelled down in hopes of a response, but even as he did so, he knew none would come. Instead he heard a soft, ominous, moaning sound rising from the depths below. Startled, Traveler took a step back. The old man didn't know what he was hearing, but he was certain the sound wasn't uttered by anything human.

The crack itself was massive in its width. Three of the Head Man's huts, lying side by side, would not have reached across to the far side. Rescuing those on the other side would be a challenging problem indeed. Traveler didn't think it was possible.

One of the villagers called out to those trapped on the far ledge of the fissure, "I don't think we can reach you. You need to try and climb out on your side. If you can, follow the crack toward the river. Maybe you can find a fallen brown nut tree to cross!"

Unbeknownst to those gathered with the old man along the near edge of the fissure, the river's water was now completely diverted from its normal channel and was now being swallowed up by the giant fissure. The river water was joined by the water still running through the village channels, which cascaded down into the crack on the upper side of the village, disappearing as well from sight far below.

Stepping back from the crack's edge, Traveler slowly looked around at the devastation. Only a few of the surviving huts were miraculously still standing. Most of the mud roofs had collapsed inward, while others had been crushed by splintered trees or fallen branches.

'*What could be done?*' The old man glanced again down into the crack as his mind sought an answer.

Onyx and Violeta rushed from their undamaged hut over to where Traveler was standing.

"Are you hurt?" they both asked the old man as one.

"No, I'm fine. But we have to try and help these people. Quick! Get the hide ropes you made and try to help these people climb out of there." Onyx turned to sprint back to his cabin as Traveler yelled at his back. "Hurry, the crack is beginning to steam!"

Traveler looked down into the crack at the small width of land clinging to the far wall. He wondered what was holding it there?

Traveler thought to himself, '*Would the ropes be long enough to reach them? Even if the ropes did reach, could those being rescued hold on when they crashed into the near wall of the crack? Would the new ropes even hold their weight?*' These were all questions the old man couldn't answer.

As Traveler watched, a few more survivors began to emerge from beneath the rubble of their collapsed huts clinging to the fissure's far wall. They frantically looked for a way to safety, but the sheer walls of the crack easily prevented their escape.

Steam began to rise thicker from the fissure's depths. Those trapped became hysterical in their frightened panic. With the heat in the fissure climbing quickly, they began clawing at the shear wall in their desperate efforts to escape. All the time, the mist from the steam continued to grow thicker and hotter. It was now so thick it was becoming difficult to even see those trapped below.

As Onyx rushed from his hut with the braided leather rope, Emma again emerged right after him frantically screaming a second warning to those gathered at the crack's edge, "Get back! Get away from the crack! Run!"

As she continued to scream her warning to run, an ominous rumbling emitted from deep within the crack below. Those who had gathered at the fissure's edge, hearing the strange girl's warning again, along with the crack's menacing rumbling, turned to run from the edge in panic. Within moments an explosive jet of scalding water erupted up and down the crack's length. Many villagers screamed with pain as those not quick enough to react to Emma's warning were showered with scalding water.

Like a few others, Traveler too had reacted slowly to Emma's cries of warning. Onyx and Violeta had literally yanked the old man off his feet as they rushed him away from the fissure. Only because of their quick reactions were they able to avoid the water and steam jetting up from the gaping void's depths that severely burned anyone who remained within its reach. As the eruption subsided to thick rising steam, the old man did not have to look back to know the fate of those poor unfortunates that had been trapped below. They were gone. He knew, no one could have survived such a continuous jet of scalding steam and water. A few moments later, the jets of scalding water subsided almost as quickly as they had appeared.

The few villagers who now took the risk of moving closer to look through the diminishing steam for their loved ones below, let out anguished cries and fell to their knees in grief upon the wet earth. Nothing was left within the crack. The ledge of ground upon which the ruined huts and momentary survivors had once stood had given way, vanishing into the depths below.

Traveler adjusted his cape and hat and cautiously moved forward as well. Once again he had dropped his walking staff, and he didn't want to lose it. With the trading of the rock-that-looks-back, the staff was now the only thing of value he possessed. Fear of losing the staff was greater than the fear he felt emanating from the crack. He scanned the area and was relieved to see the staff lying in the mud near the edge of the crack. He quickly moved forward to retrieve it before quickly backing away again.

All around him, Traveler saw villagers being treated for their burns suffered by the eruption of scalding water. Some had been luckier than others, having already dawned their caps and capes to work in the fields. Others were not so lucky, and suffered greatly with severe burns. He didn't think a few would see the sunrise of another day.

As Traveler surveyed the village he saw the Head Man pushing and clawing his way out from beneath the ruins of his collapsed hut. Traveler quickly turned back to Violeta and Onyx, standing nearby in stunned awe.

Nodding towards the Head Man's hut, Traveler urgently warned, "Violeta, hurry. Hide Emma."

As Violeta quickly hustled Emma away, Traveler, with Onyx's assistance, turned and began to limp over in the Head Man's direction. They arrived just as Bobane worked his last foot free from the ruins of his collapsed hut and cautiously stood up.

The Head Man rubbed the dust and dirt from his head and face and re-adjusted his eye-slits. He rubbed the back of his head again before holding his hand up to his eye-slits to look for any blood. Satisfied at the absence of blood, Bobane looked around at his ruined village. He paused a moment to stare at the steam still rising from the crack before his attention turned to the two men standing before him.

The Head Man's blank stare made Traveler feel a little anxious. He was standing a polite distance in front of Bobane with Onyx a few steps behind. Traveler politely bowed his head again as the Head man continued to stare blankly at them. Onyx did not, he just glared back at Bobane. As the Head Man's stare began to show signs of recognition, Traveler enquired, "Are you all right?"

"Traveler? Is that you, Traveler?"

Before the old man could reply, The Head man mumbled, "What happened?"

"We had a ground shake," Traveler replied. "You must have been knocked unconscious when your hut collapsed. The ground shake caused this huge crack to open through the village. Everybody caught on the far side of the crack has been lost."

Bobane stared questioningly at Traveler, trying to comprehend the old man's words. After a few moments, Bobane's eyes widened and his forehead wrinkled above his eye-slits, as his mind slowly began to comprehend what Traveler was telling him. He turned his head to stare over again at the steaming crack.

"The huts on that side of the village were mainly my clan. Smokey Mountain Clan; my people," Bobane mumbled in shock.

"Luckily, most of the villagers had already gone to the fields," Traveler replied.

Bobane looked back a moment at Traveler, before starting to take a few steps in the fissure's direction to see for himself. Traveler hesitated before cautiously following the Head Man a few steps behind. Onyx stayed behind.

"The crack has severed all the channels, the village is lost." The old man pointed toward the cascading water above, as the Head Man continued to walk closer to the steaming crack to see for himself.

Traveler warned, "I wouldn't get too close. It could erupt again."

Just as Traveler cautioned Bobane, a soft rumbling emitted from deep within the bowel's of the crack. Upon hearing this ominous sound, the Head Man stopped, heeding the old man's warning. He quickly backed up, his head turning as his eyes followed the crack away from the village center before stopping to stare at the water cascading into the crack from the closest of the severed water channels.

As the two men stood there considering what to do, the villagers that had been working in the fields began to arrive back at the village. Very few had been injured, but there had been two killed by falling trees. They streamed in, searching for their loved ones. The village square erupted in cries of joy or screams of grief as they learned the fate of their families.

Amongst all this chaos, Bobane finally turned back to Traveler and mumbled under his breath, "What do we do now? Without the channels, the ratta will overrun us."

Traveler had not considered this before. His mind had been totally focused on trying to save the trapped villagers. After a few moments, the old man quietly replied, "I suggest any survivors not seriously injured should gather all the food and supplies we can save and move up into the brown nut trees down by the river."

The Head Man began to noticeably nod his head in agreement as he considered Traveler's suggestion. Bobane called to two nearby men as they ran in from the fields. They ignored his words and began to frantically dig through the ruins of a nearby hut. Bobane called for two others, standing a short distance away, and beckoned them over. They turned to see who called, before slowly walking over.

"You two, I need you to check the outer water channel and see if it can be salvaged." The men started to protest, looking a moment back at the village, but when they saw Bobane's hand reach down for the handle of his club, they turned toward the fields and jogged away to fulfill the Head Man's request.

It didn't take long before the two returned. One of them stepped forward to report the bad news. "Most of the water channels still have a little water flowing. But, we don't think it's enough to stop the ratta. Some big trees have also fallen across the channels as well. They're too big to move and a couple have partially dammed and diverted the channels. It would take a couple of moons to dig new channels around all the fallen trees. For now, the ratta have numerous bridges to cross. We don't see anyway of stopping them."

After delivering the bad news, the two men hurried off to tend to their own families. Traveler walked over to the Head Man's side. "I heard what he said. Even if the channels could be repaired, there's no certainty that the ratta couldn't come from the crack's side. We know they're dam good climbers. There's also a good chance some fallen trees might have bridged the crack itself. Especially down by the river where the big brown nut trees are. If there's a way in, the ratta will find it."

The Head Man rubbed the back of his head as he thought, and re-adjusted his eye slits. Searching for a solution, Bobane suggested, "Perhaps, we can move the village upriver and dig new channels. The ground there is rockier and it would take a long time, but I don't see any other options. We might even be able to include some of the existing outer fields by changing the channels some." He looked to the old man for confirmation. "What do you think?"

"I don't think it can be done." Traveler slowly shook his head. "It took many generations to dig the current channels and clear the existing fields of rocks. You just said so yourself, the ground is even rockier the further up-river we go. I don't see how it can be done."

Traveler took in a deep breath before stating his proposal. "You just have to move the village. Start over. There has to be a better spot, and I think I know where."

Traveler paused for a moment to let his words sink in. "I think you have to accept the fact that this village is doomed. In the meantime, it would be wise to have any women and children not injured to begin harvesting anything they can from the fields and take them to the brown nut trees," Traveler suggested. "With no water to stop them the ratta will feast tonight on anything left behind in the fields."

The Head Man paused in thought for a moment. He then began to nod several times in agreement before turning to a man tightly holding his injured arm walking nearby. "Ort, I need you to organize the women and children and start harvesting anything ripe enough to eat. Take whatever you gather to the brown nuttrees down by the river."

"Wait!" Traveler blurted out. "I just realized. We can't do that. We can't take all the food up in the trees. There wouldn't be enough room for the villagers." The old man noticed the Head Man's anger growing from being contradicted, and quickly suggested, "Perhaps any crops we gather might be stored in one of the huts? If we cover it with poles, brush, and rocks, it might be enough to keep the ratta out."

"That just might work," Bobane replied. "My hut is the biggest and most of the side poles and walls are still standing. I'll get some men to start cleaning out the collapsed roof and we'll use it to store what we can,".

Turning back to Ort, Bobane directed, "You heard Traveler. Bring anything harvested to my hut and we'll store it there."

The Head Man turned to Traveler and said, "I'll give some thought to what you said; about moving the village."

Bobane then began issuing other directives, many with the old man's advice, and the villagers set about fulfilling their given tasks. Some were sent to build nests high up in the trees for the villagers to sleep on, while others began removing the debris from the collapsed roof of the Head Man's hut. Nearby fallen branches as well as building materials from other collapsed huts were collected to help in covering the gathered harvest that would be stored there.

Hindering the villagers, throughout the long afternoon and into the night, was the crack that ran through the village. The huts nearest the fissure were unusable. Their past inhabitants were terrified even to go near. Steam continuously emitted from the depths of the ripped earth. Periodically without warning, the crack rumbled and small eruptions of scalding water and steam jetted forth from below.

As Traveler moved about the ruined village he could easily see the fear on some of the older villager's faces. They knew what was coming. They had all heard the stories of when The People lived in the trees at the mercy of the ratta. Without having to utter a word, they dreaded the thought of going back to enduring those starving times and living in the trees. Yes, they knew the stories all too well. This fear drove them to work that much harder to protect anything they could from the dreaded ratta.

Traveler made his rounds amongst the villagers, quietly spreading the word, with those who had expressed a desire to join him, that he still planned to leave on the second sunrise and to prepare accordingly. Some told the old man they were reconsidering because of injured family members. Traveler responded that he understood their dilemma and promised to help with their injured anyway he could. He tried hard to convince them of what he knew; that the village was lost and could not be saved. He tried to explain that staying behind was unfortunately no longer a viable option. Some just shrugged their shoulders in defeat and shook their heads. A few just said they had to stay, they had no other choice. They would try to follow at a later time. Maybe the rainy moons when the ratta would not be a threat. "Perhaps you could mark the trail somehow?"

"It wouldn't do any good. You wouldn't be able to find us," the old man warned. "A small group won't survive in the wilds if you get lost," he warned as he walked away.

Throughout the rest of the day, the villagers gathered what they could salvage of their own food supplies and other items of need and prepared to move up into the trees. Ratta hide bags stuffed with smoked ratta meat, dried fruit, nuts, and some of the harvested vegetables were hung from branches high up into the trees, out of reach of any marauding ratta who would come with the dark. Whatever was saved from the fields was taken to be stored in the Head Man's hut, covered with brush and rocks.

Since most of the villagers had never slept in a tree before, they were uncertain and anxious with the upcoming prospect. Traveler gathered a few of the younger men and instructed them in the art of building a simple sleeping nest. Under the old man's watchful eye, they gathered fallen branches and began to wedge and weave them between tree limbs to form a simple nest. He then showed them how to fill this platform with grass and leaves to make a fairly comfortable bed to sleep on. Granted, not as comfortable as their mud huts, but at least safer from the marauding ratta. He in turn, asked those villagers to help others construct their nests.

As night approached, Traveler gathered all the villagers together to try and ease their fears of the upcoming night. "Look at me! I'm an old man and I fight the ratta every night I'm on a journey. If an old man like me can do it with one arm, then you can too. Just stay calm and alert and you'll be OK." He then went on to explain just what to expect. "After they attack, and you defeat them, they will not return. Then you can rest. Before that, I suggest you remain vigilant. They always attack at midnight, but if you are caught sleeping, it could be fatal. So, stay awake until after they attack. Have your spears and clubs ready, for they will surely come."

chapter fourteen

"The River"

Dreaded darkness fell ominously over the village that night. The villagers had prepared, as best they could, for what Traveler told them was coming, but it wasn't enough. Having lived for generations in the relative safety the water channels provided, they simply underestimated the numbers of ratta that would cross over the damaged water channels on the newly fallen trees.

First, the ratta ate everything in the outer fields the villagers had been unable to harvest the previous day. It was not enough. The ratta turned their attention on the village, drawn by the overpowering scent of human blood.

Three brave, elderly men had volunteered to remain behind in the village. They took shelter in Violeta and Onyx's hut, since it had suffered very little damage during the ground shake. The three men were there to protect four severely injured villagers who lay on the earthen benches along the hut's walls. With the severity of their injuries it had been impossible to raise them into the safety of the trees. The men, had armed themselves with spears and clubs, in an attempt to protect the injured. The villagers had fortified the hut as strong as they could, both inside and out. The newly constructed log door was braced from within and brush and wood were piled thickly around the outside of the hut's walls and roof in hopes of preventing the ratta's entry. Relatives and friends of the injured offered their thanks and well wishes to the volunteers before retreating to the brown nut trees.

Traveler knew first hand the futility of their efforts and pleaded with the villagers not to leave their loved ones to the mercy of the ratta. He suggested unsuccessfully, it would be more merciful to suffocate the severely injured in order to assist their spirit's passing to the Spirit World. He tried his best to warn the volunteer guards that the ratta were too strong and numerous and would stop at nothing once they scented human blood. But, the villagers would not listen, for they had not seen the power of the ratta as the storyteller had. Plus, they had faith in their efforts to fortify the hut. The ratta had no way in.

Those sheltering in the brown nut trees that night had to endure the screams of pain and shrieks of battle emanating from the nearby hut. Fortunately, they didn't have to listen for long, for the ratta were numerous and the hut suddenly fell silent. The only sounds those closest to the hut heard then, were the ratta's snarling as they fought over a choice piece of meat.

The terrified villagers sat quietly in the trees, whispering amongst themselves. They relived the screams of their friends in their mind, all the while wondering, was this to be their fate? *'Would they be next?'* They didn't have to wait long. Looking down from their nests, they watched as he ratta began to gather around the tree trunks. The ratta squabbled and jostled amongst themselves as they stared excitedly up at their victims high in the trees.

Nobody was aware when it actually occurred, except maybe Emma, but it happened sometime during the night. Perhaps even during the period of time the villagers were battling the ratta in the brown nut trees. The nearby river abruptly stopped flowing. An eerie quiet blanketed the land as the soft rumblings ceased coming from the fissure as well.

The following morning, after surviving their own battles with the ratta, some of the villagers gathered below Mother's brown nut tree. Traveler had asked the villagers who planned to leave with him on the following morning to meet him there one hand past sunrise. They were talking quietly amongst themselves as they waited for the old man to join them. Most still carried their bloody spears and clubs they had used to battle the ratta the previous night. They were nervous and reluctant to set the bloody weapons aside, never having survived such a night before.

Some of those gathered were having second thoughts about their decisions to leave. They were scared. The ground shake disaster that struck the village the previous day had resulted in the deaths of many, and left few families intact without serious injuries to loved ones. There was great concern over those loved ones whose bodies had not been recovered. *'Could their shadow spirit's pass over to the Spirit World without undergoing the Shadow Spirit Dance or would those become tormented spirits, trapped forever between the two worlds?'*

Tensions were mounting. What had started out as quiet discussions were beginning to become heated exchanges between those determined to go and those looking for an excuse to stay. Those still determined to leave felt betrayed by those now wishing to stay.

It was at that moment Bobane noticed the group and walked over to see what was going on. Most of those gathered grew quiet when they saw the Head Man approaching. However, the two villagers arguing about the group's decision to leave the following morning had not noticed Bobane's approach and he overheard their heated exchange about leaving.

"What's this talk about leaving?" Bobane demanded in an obvious challenge, his hand moving to rest on the handle of his bloody club hanging from his waist.

"Who's leaving!" the Head Man yelled. "You? You?" He shouted as he glared at each of those gathered in turn. "The elders and I make those decisions, not you!"

Those gathered stood quietly, afraid to speak, as Bobane continued to rant and confront the group. Finally, one of the two men, gripping his own bloody spear, gathered the courage to reply. He was just about to do so when he was interrupted by a voice calling down from above.

"I am! I'm leaving! And, if you're going with me, we must hurry, there isn't much time," came a girls voice calling down from above.

All heads looked up to see who had just dared to challenge Bobane's authority. What they saw was a beautiful young girl with long, flowing, golden hair. All who gazed upon her were amazed, not just because of her hair, but because of her flawless body as a whole. She stood tall, straight, and confident as she looked down on those gathered below and they stared back in awe. The villagers looking up could see no defects; no deformities at all. *'How could this be?'*

"And, just who are you, who dare to challenge me, your head man?" Bobane asked, already anticipating the answer.

"She's the same girl that warned us before the ground shake yesterday!" someone blurted out.

Another agreed. "I heard her too. She was running about yelling to get out of the huts and later to get away from the crack. She saved the lives of my family!"

"She saved my family as well," another added. "Thank you! Thank you!"

One of the other villagers softly said, "I thought she was but a vision; a gift sent by Mother Earth herself."

Others mumbled in agreement, as they stood staring up in awe.

The young girl raised a hand to speak. "My name is Emma. I have lived here with my great-grandmother since I was born. You knew her as 'Mother,'" she said.

"I thought I heard someone yelling a warning before the water and steam eruption," Bobane said. "But, I couldn't tell who it was. How could you know what was going to happen beforehand? How's that possible? Are you a goddess? Or perhaps a spirit as Diego suggested?" After a short pause he continued, "Or maybe a witch?"

"No, I'm not a god. Nor am I a witch," Emma responded. "I'm a seer, like my great-grandmother. I sometimes hear and see things in the future. Sometimes things long before they happen and other times just before they occur. Like the ground shake yesterday."

"Why have you been hiding?" Bobane demanded.

"Mother thought it best I remain unknown until I'd mastered my abilities," Emma replied. "She knew you would not understand. Mother was obviously right, since you just suggested I was a witch." The young girl paused a moment before adding, "We were also waiting for Traveler to reach the village. Mother needed to talk with him before she passed, so we joined our minds and summoned him with a shadow vision."

The gathered villagers looked from one to another in disbelief. *'How could this be possible?'* they all thought.

"What do you mean, 'you summoned him?'" Bobane asked.

"It's kinda hard to explain." Emma paused for a moment as she searched for the right words to formulate an answer. "It's kinda like sending a mental image on the wind. She and I both have known for many moons that the great southern volcano was about to erupt. We just didn't know when. We sent Traveler the mountain's image in his dreams. Great-grandmother had always told me, my mental abilities were far greater than hers. I wasn't sure what would happen, but I'm grateful he saw the smoking mountain in his dreams. Of course, Traveler could not have understood the vision he was seeing but he came anyway, out of concern for Mother."

Traveler, with another group of men, walked up to the gathering just as Emma was finishing. He immediately saw Bobane in the gathering and knew this meant trouble.

Bobane saw the old man approaching with his group a few moments later and turned to challenge him, his hand resting on the handle of his heavy club. Those who saw the Head Man's actions, tensed for a confrontation. But, before Traveler or Bobane had a chance to say anything, Emma began to shout out another warning to all those who would listen.

"Silence, silence! Nothing but silence. Do you not hear? You listen, but you do not hear!" Emma called down to those gathered below.

The men below looked from Bobane to Traveler in turn, before staring back up at Emma for answers.

"What do you mean, girl? I don't hear anything," Bobane asked.

"That's what I'm trying to tell you. All is quiet; too quiet. The river has stopped flowing," she replied from above. "We must leave this place. Now! We don't have much time."

"You can't hear the river from here."

"I can, and it's not flowing." Emma replied.

"That's not possible," Bobane said before turning to one of the gathered men. "Boon, run down to the river and see what's happening."

The Head Man turned to Traveler. "You lied to me old man. Emma has been here all the time, and you've known it!" Bobane's hand closed around the handle of his heavy club and he withdrew it from his waistband. "No one lies to me and lives to do it a second time!" Bobane sneered, "Especially not an old story telling fool like you."

As Bobane began to raise the club, three men sprang forward, leveling their spears at the Head Man's chest.

"If anyone's going to die, it'll be you!" Onyx threatened, as he pulled Traveler behind him and forced the Head Man to step back with the tip of his fire-hardened spear point.

Bobane glared at Onyx and the two other spear holders who dared to challenge him. He stepped back another step as he slid his club back into his waistband. "I'll deal with you later, old man." Turning to face Onyx and the other two men who had stepped up, he added, "Same goes for you three; this ain't over."

"I look forward to it," Onyx replied.

Staring up at Emma, Bobane ordered, "Girl, get down here now! You're coming with me."

"I think Emma can make up her own mind as to where she wants to go," Traveler quietly said. "And, I think she's already made that decision pretty clear."

Seeing he was powerless to do anything about it at the moment, Bobane turned and stormed off in anger. "We'll see about that!" He yelled back threateningly over his shoulder.

A few moments later the runner came back from the river.

"She's right, the river's stopped flowing! The river terror's are feasting on the fish and serpents still left in the puddles."

Emma heard the runner's words and called down to those gathered. "We don't have much time, we have to cross the river now! Right now!"

"Are you sure, Emma?" Traveler asked. "Some may not be ready."

"Yes, and we don't have much time, the water will return!" she warned all who would listen.

"You heard her," Traveler yelled. "If you want to live, gather your families and whatever supplies you can and head to the river! Do it now!"

The gathered men turned and jogged off to other brown nut trees to gather their families and supplies. "Hurry!" Emma yelled to the backs of the men jogging away.

Traveler stayed behind with Emma, where he had spent the previous night. He quickly began gathering his own meager supplies together.

Word spread quickly throughout the villagers of the mystical girl's warning, and that Traveler's group was leaving right now. Luckily, those already planning to join him the following morning were already packed. They quickly gathered their supplies and began making their way back to Mother's brown nut tree. A few of those gathering below the tree carried injured family members on their backs. Except for the very young, even the children carried what they could.

Traveler had supervised the construction of two litters made from portions of the great hide, that had not been braided into lengths of rope, and he pointed to the two most gravely wounded to be placed on the litters. Four men volunteered to be litter bearers and at Emma's urging they quickly set off towards the river.

As most of the villagers gathered to leave, the others stood watching. They were mainly members of the Smokey Mountain Clan and had no knowledge of the Rushing River Clan's imminent departure. As their numbers grew they became more belligerent towards the other group gathering at the base of Mother's tree.

Some of the angry villagers who were being left behind approached Traveler as he organized those about to depart.

"Why were we not informed of your leaving?" one demanded in anger. "Does Bobane know?"

"He does now. Our leaving was planned days before yesterday's disaster," the old man replied. "But now things have taken a change for the worse. This village cannot be saved. If you wish to join us, you are welcome to do so. We are leaving now though. Gather what supplies you can carry and follow us if you like. But, if you choose to follow, you must hurry. Emma predicts the water will be coming back. We are heading towards the bright star and will mark our route with piled rocks."

While what remained of the Smokey Mountain Clan watched, Emma and Traveler began to lead the column of those leaving down toward the river bed. As the old man had insisted, all but the very youngest of those setting off carried a spear or had a club tucked into their waistband. Everyone capable carried ratta hide packs full of dried ratta, fruit, or vegetables, as well as their water skins.

Traveler followed a few steps behind Emma. He was pleased to see the new cap, cape, and sandals Violeta had made for her sister. She had sized them from Mother's cape and cap, passing down Mother's elaborate design intact in the center of the cape. The design featured a giant eye radiating beams of sunlight in all directions. The old man thought that was only fitting.

When the column approached the river bank Emma turned back to urge the group to hurry before she descended down the steep bank and immediately out onto the muddy river bed. Traveler's eyes opened wider under his eye-slit as he recognized the shadow vision from his dreams two nights before. The shadow vision standing on the river bank, was indeed Emma.

'How could this be?' he thought to himself.

The column came to a halt as the people bunched together at the top of the river bank and stared out over the muddy river bed. Traveler could see the anxiety in their eyes as they watched the river terrors gorging themselves on the dying fish just a short distance away. He also saw Bobane leading an armed group of men leaving the village a short distance away. They didn't appear to be carrying anything but clubs.

"We need to cross quick," Traveler said. "We have trouble coming!"

Emma had walked right by one of the river terrors as it feasted and she turned to yell back at the frightened villagers still hesitating on the river bank.

"You must hurry!" she yelled back in encouragement. "Don't be afraid, the river terrors will not harm you!"

"We have to cross right now! There's no time to waste." Traveler said as he descended down the river bank and out onto the mud. "Emma has not been wrong before. Hurry if you want to live!"

Onyx and Violeta, along with their children, were the first to follow the old man out onto the muddy river bed. They were quickly followed by the rest of those gathered. They weaved their way around and between river terrors who watched them with large, yellow eyes as they passed. Only once did one of the monsters lunge at a passing villager who came too close. Fortunately, the beast was slowed by a swollen stomach and the giant jaws snapped together on empty air as the startled villager leapt away unscathed.

The villagers were only half way across when Emma once again turned back to urge the group to move more urgently. "Hurry," she yelled. "The water is coming! I have seen it!"

The villagers all turned to look upstream, expecting to see water. But, they saw nothing; they heard nothing.

Emma had already made it to the top of the opposite river bank when she turned again. She saw Bobane's men beginning to descend the far river bank, but she was not concerned with them. She already knew they were doomed. She issued a more empathic warning.

"Run!" Emma yelled. "If you want to live, run! Get to the trees! The water is coming!"

Emma ran back down the steep bank when she saw Traveler struggling up the steep embankment. As they reached the bank's top, a horrendous explosion issued forth from deep within the canyon above the log jam Traveler had last crossed.

"Run!" Emma yelled down at those beginning to climb out of the muddy river bed. "To the brown nut trees. Run!"

The villagers didn't need to hear Emma's warning again. Now they could easily hear the crashes and terrifying roar echoing down the canyon's steep granite walls a short distance upriver. Although they could not yet see it, a wall of water as high as the tallest brown nut tree was rushing down the narrow canyon, destroying everything in its path. The huge log jam and rock slide, far up the river's canyon that had been blocking the river's flow, had finally given way to the tremendous pressure of the water building up behind it.

As soon as Emma's group of villagers reached the brown nut trees, a short distance beyond the river bank, they began to climb in panic. Upriver, a tremendous explosion of water and debris smashed through the log jam at the opening of the canyon. The water burst through the narrow opening at such tremendous pressure, that a plume of water shot a hundred paces downriver. Debris laden, muddy water quickly overflowed the river's bed and spread across the valley floor. Within minutes the surrounding country, as far as the eye could see, was covered in water. When the old man saw the rushing water, he didn't think he was going to make it! He was uttering a prayer to Mother Earth when the wave of water washed over him.

Traveler awoke to find himself securely wedged in a crook of the tree, halfway up a brown nut tree. This puzzled him since the last thing he remembered before the water smashed into him was he was just starting his climb at the base of the tree.

"I'm glad to see you awake. I wasn't sure you were going to make it. I grabbed you just as the water hit," Onyx called down from above. Traveler look up towards the sound of the voice and saw Emma, Violeta and the children sitting next to Onyx.

Traveler looked around in a sudden panic. "Where's my walking staff?" he frantically asked. "For the love of the Gods, please tell me you have it!"

"I'm sorry, Traveler. The water took it as I was pulling you to safety," Onyx replied. "We'll find you something else you can use."

"You don't understand. That walking staff has been passed down from my great-grandfather, and maybe generations before him. I have to find it." The old man was in a panic as he started to climb down the tree.

"You can't look now, the water's still over your head," Violeta called down. "We're stuck here for a while, that's for sure."

"What about Bobane, did any of them make it?"

"No, they were in the center of the river bed when the wave of water and logs overtook them. Nobody could have survived," Onyx replied. "Nobody knows about any of those left on the far side of the river. I suppose some of them may have survived, but I'm pretty sure the log-jam crossing point is probably gone now anyway. Nobody could cross the river now if they wanted to."

"What about our group? Did we loose anyone?"

"Yes, we think we lost maybe two hands of people, but that's just a guess. Mainly the injured and elderly that weren't fast enough to reach the safety of the trees in time. We also lost two young ones. They were still too low in the branches when they were ripped from their mother's arms by the initial wave of water that washed over us," Violeta informed Traveler. "We'll just have to wait to see who survived for sure once the water recedes."

A lump was developing in his throat as Traveler listened to the details of the disaster. He felt selfish and awful being so concerned with his staff when so many of the villagers had lost their lives. Villagers he had personally persuaded to follow him to a better life and now felt responsible for their deaths.

Onyx called down from above, "I saw many people drop everything in their frantic efforts to reach the trees once they saw the water. I watched both litters being swept away with their occupants when they were dropped by the litter bearers in their haste to reach the trees. I don't think any of them made it. They were too far behind. We've lost most of our supplies. We're in real serious trouble."

"Not a very auspicious start to our journey," Traveler replied under his breath, stating the obvious.

As the villagers sat in the trees waiting for the water to recede, the great soarers filled the sky as dusk set in. The People watched night after night as the soarers dived down to pick unwary ratta from the tree tops where they had sought safety from the water. It was almost a hand of days before the water receded enough to allow the most desperate of the villagers to safely climb down from the trees. Some, isolated in trees where there had been little or no food were literally starving. Generous villagers shared what food they had with others in their tree, but the food was unable to reach all. The water had been too high and swift.

Although they had not seen any in the area, Traveler cautioned those descending to be wary of any river terrors that may have survived the flooding. The water was still knee deep when Traveler cautiously joined the first frantic group of villagers to descend. Those who had food, shared with the hungry who came to beg. Others immediately began searching for their loved ones, praying for some miracle whereas they might have survived the flood. A few more practical searched for supplies that might have been caught up in branches or brush downriver.

The searchers were unsuccessful. They encountered no river terrors, nor did they find any human remains, or packs. What they did find though, were ratta. Dead ratta, caught up in bushes as well as lower tree limbs. The villagers even spotted a few younger ratta, that had survived the flood waters by climbing the trees. They had somehow avoided the nightly hunts of the great soarers above, and now stared hungrily down at the human searchers that waded in the water below. But the ratta were helpless to attack since their great fear of water deterred any urge they might have had.

Traveler searched as well. He searched downriver not for bodies, packs, or ratta; he searched for his walking staff. He already knew, deep down, that the staff was lost to him, but he refused to give up hope. So he searched anyway. The old man felt he was in good graces with Mother Earth and the gods and he too was hoping for a miracle.

Agonizing in his mind for the last five days and sleepless nights over what he would say to his father and grandfathers when they reunited in the Spirit World made Traveler frantic. He knew his time of passing was drawing near and he was growing more and more anxious. *'What words could he possibly say to his ancestors that could ease his guilt? Nothing; there was nothing he could say.'*

When the searchers made their way back to the other villagers empty handed, they just shook their heads in defeat and disappointment. Traveler returned a short time later, but unlike the others, he was not empty handed. He was carrying four dead ratta. As he approached the trees, he held them up.

He yelled up to the villagers sitting in the branches above, "If you want to live, go and find as many ratta as you can. We'll cut the meat in strips and sun dry them in the tree branches."

For the next three days, the ratta strips dried in the tree branches. The hides were dried as well, and the women gathered to sew them into bags to carry the newly dried ratta. Other ratta hides were used to replace lost capes to shelter from the suns fierce heat.

The group finally resumed their interrupted journey on the fourth morning. Once they were able to reach each villager they were able to determine how many were lost to the flood, and their numbers were staggering. They had lost more than half of their initial group to the river's flood. Only five hands and two continued. Emma walked a few paces behind Traveler as they waded in the ankle-deep water across the valley. Traveler was assisted with a new walking staff Onyx had presented to him just before they set out.

"I know it's not as nice as your old staff, but I hope it will suffice."

"Thank you, Onyx. I'm sure it will do the job. I appreciate it," Traveler told his friend, while inside his heart ached.

chapter fifteen

"Scar's Surprise"

The sun was three hands high when Traveler led the small group up and out of the valley floor. They had left the water behind a short time ago and were relieved to finally be walking on grassy, muddy ground. The old man insisted they all take a long drink of water and refill their water skins before they left the soggy land behind. They then began the slow, steep, climb to the pass above where they would finally leave their once beautiful valley behind. Other than Traveler, none of the group had ever been out of the valley. Only a few had even been across the river. Everything was new, and they were edgy and tense. Their fate lay now in the hands of an old storyteller and a mysterious girl they had only met a few days ago. Turning back was no longer an option; crossing the river was impossible. Their only option now was to continue on.

In single file the small group followed Traveler's lead. As they walked, they chewed on dried ratta from the flood. Ten days had passed since they left their valley and the villagers were becoming trail hardened. They had been lucky so far, since the great flood they had not suffered any serious injuries on their journey other than a couple of sprained ankles. Everybody had a few bumps and bruises, as well as scratches from the cactus, but that was to be expected. No one complained. Even Traveler's head had healed and his legs had regained their strength.

Traveler took his bearings nightly, locating the brightest star and then waiting for sun rise to double-check his route. Emma had not questioned Traveler's choice of direction. The old man was still following faint trails he was familiar with from past journeys. He was somewhat relieved to easily recognize various landmarks. He had been somewhat concerned that his mind might play tricks on him again. Even with the blistering sun beating down on them, they pushed on, resting only for a couple of hands at mid day.

It was while they were resting at mid day that Emma came over and sat down beside him.

"How are you holding up, Emma?" the old man asked, wiping the sweat from his eyes with the edge of his cape, before readjusting his eye slits.

"I'm fine." She took off her eye-slits and dropped them to dangle on her chest. She paused a moment before smiling and leaned over to him to whisper, "I have a surprise for you. Scar is watching us."

"What! Where?"

"He's just beyond the distant tree line; in the shadows," Emma pointed. "I saw her in my dreams a few nights ago, but didn't realize what I was seeing. There's five of them and they've been following us since daybreak. I didn't want to say anything until I was certain."

Traveler stared but couldn't see any movement in the direction she pointed.

"I don't see a thing," he said, discouraged. Looking at the young girl he asked, "How can you see anything without your eye-slits?"

"I don't need them, I never wore them in the tree. They don't seem to help. You must have forgotten, I'm a little different than the rest of you. I can't see anything in the dark. I only wear eye-slits now so the villagers won't think I'm a witch."

"Do you think I should walk over there?" Traveler nodded in the direction she had indicated.

"I don't think so, since she's not alone," she replied. "She'll come to you when she's ready."

Traveler gathered the weary travelers together when they stopped for the day under a stand of brown nut trees. Emma stood beside him as he cautioned them about the four-legged animals that are undoubtedly watching them at this vary moment.

"I don't feel any threat emanating from the beasts at all, just a sense of curiosity," Emma quickly added.

"I wanted to tell everyone since I don't want any of you to feel threatened and throw a spear, or rock at them if they do come near to visit." The old man continued, "They're being cautious, and I don't want them scared. They may be able to assist us. They've been following us since early morning. If they were going to attack, they probably would have done so by now, but if you or your family feel nervous, you should climb to your nests early."

"Traveler and I will sit for a while, a little ways off, hoping Scar will find her courage for a visit," Emma added.

Traveler and Emma didn't have to wait long before the old man was re-united with his old friend, Scar. Yes, he didn't wait long, but he was surprised!

The four legged beast cautiously moved forward soon after they sat down on a fallen tree trunk. Steadily eyeing Emma as he approached, Scar stopped a few feet in front of her old friend and promptly dropped Traveler's staff at his feet. The animal backed up a few paces and sank to the ground. Scar stared at the staff and then up at Traveler. She let out a little whining sound when the old man didn't react. She again stared at the staff she had just dropped before gazing again at the old man.

After the initial shock wore off, Traveler finally reached down and retrieved the family heirloom. Bringing it up close to his face, he examined it carefully. The center appeared to be well chewed, with teeth marks up and down the shaft, but to Traveler, it was perfect. His eye-slit fell to his chest as he wiped away the tears that streamed down his cheeks. He then reached out his hand in the beast's direction in thanks.

Scar rose up and moved cautiously forward. She reached out and licked the old man's hand in greeting. Traveler slowly moved his hand forward and gently touched the top of Scar's head. He then slowly pulled his hand back and reached in his bag behind him for a piece of dried ratta. He offered the dried meat to his four legged friend. Scar stepped forward and gently took the offered meat, and the old man reached forward again and scratched behind her ears.

Scar quickly backed away from his touch, turned and jogged off into the falling dusk. Traveler was worried that maybe he had scared her away with his touch. But, Scar was not gone long before she returned, closely followed by her four pups. One pup was almost as large as its mother. All four sank down a few paces behind her, in front of the two humans and watched.

Emma immediately offered her hand out, palm up, holding another small piece of dried ratta.

"Don't look in her eyes, lower your gaze in submission," Traveler suggested.

Emma lowered her gaze to stare at the ground in front of her and quietly waited. She held her offering steady for such a long time that her arm was beginning to ache. Finally, her perseverance was rewarded. To their surprise, Scar gave a little whine, and the largest of the pups rose and cautiously stepped forward. The animal took a quick sniff of the offering, then gently snatched it from the girl's hand before quickly moving back to sink down again behind his mother.

"Good boy," she said softly.

Emma looked over at Traveler and beamed excitedly. "It looks like maybe I've made a friend, as well," she whispered.

However, her soft words did not register with the old man. He was too engrossed in studying the staff, holding it close to his eyes as he slowly turned it over and over in his hands; examining every bit of its surface in detail.

Not wishing to interrupt her old friend's concentration, Emma withdrew another piece of dried meat from her bag, and once again reached it out in offering to the beasts lying in front of them. This time, the big pup stood instantly, and immediately stepped forward to gently take the offering of meat from the girl's open hand. Unlike the first time, after gulping down the treat, the animal remained standing in front of her, intently watching her every move. She slowly reached her hand out again, palm up, and the pup leaned forward to sniff her hand. The pup licked her palm and a soft whine emanated from his chest. He stared at the girl a moment before his tongue licked his snout and his head quickly nodded in her direction. He then calmly sat down on his haunches as if to say, *'I'd like another piece, please.'*

"Looks like you'd like some more," she quietly stated the obvious. She reached back into her bag and pulled out some more dried ratta. She gave another piece to the big pup seated before her, and then tossed pieces of meat to Scar and the other three pups in turn. The pups all rose as one, sniffed the pieces of meat tossed to them before picking the dried meat up to gulp down.

Emma's words and action broke Traveler's concentration and he looked up from the staff. He was somewhat startled to see the big pup patiently sitting in front of Emma. He was even more surprised to note that the animal's hide was covered in fine, short hair. He quickly turned his attention to the three other pups from Scar's litter. Traveler quickly ascertained that the big pup sitting before Emma was male, but he wasn't so sure about the other three. He suspected all three were female due to the size difference with the one in front, but time would tell. Two of the three pups, had patches of hair about their shoulders and head, while the third appeared to be hairless, like her mother.

"Looks like you've made a friend," the old man said, repeating the words Emma had stated just a short time before.

Emma laughed at his remark. "That's what I just said!"

"You'd better be careful how much ratta you give 'em," Traveler cautioned. "You need to eat yourself."

Looking around at the growing gloom of darkness falling, Traveler warned, "We'd better go and look for a tree to sleep in before it gets too dark for you to see."

As soon as the old man stood, the four pups bolted for the nearby forest. Emma watched as the largest pup stopped short of the forest and turned momentarily to look back, before trotting slowly into the shadows.

"Did you see that?" she said excitedly. "He paused to look back at me!"

Traveler didn't have the heart to tell her the pup was probably looking back at his mother. Like the big pup, he was somewhat surprised when Scar didn't run as well when they stood. She simply stood and watched as they walked past her toward the brown nut trees. It was only when they had passed her a number of paces, that she turned and trotted away in her pup's direction.

Emma walked by Traveler's side, excitedly chattering about their experience, while hanging onto the old man's arm. He carried his newly recovered staff listening to the young girl's excitement. Both had smiles spreading from ear to ear.

When they reached the trunk of the brown nut tree they planned to sleep in, Traveler turned to Emma and stated, "Did you know, that's the very first time Scar has ever allowed me to touch her since I nursed her back to life." As if an afterthought he asked, "How could Scar have found my staff? How could that be possible unless the Mother Earth or the god's intervened?"

"Perhaps they did," Emma said. "Or, maybe it's fate. All part of the plan the Gods have laid out for your life."

"Hmm, maybe," he replied.

They began to climb. Climbing was becoming difficult for Traveler, so Onyx came down to give him a hand.

Traveler's concern about Emma running out of meat vanished when they began to descend from the tree the following morning. Lying at the base of their brown nut tree lay three plump ratta. The five, four legged animals, were lying in the grass a short distance away. They watched intently as the humans descended from the trees.

"Do you think it's safe for us to climb down?" Onyx asked nervously.

"Yes, I think so," the old man replied. "Just don't make any aggressive movements or loud noises and I think you'll be just fine."

Traveler was excited but not that surprised when he stepped back on solid ground and saw the three ratta lying in the grass at the base of the brown nut tree.

"Scar always brought me a ratta each morning when we journeyed together," Traveler said as he held a plump ratta up by its bare tail. "Looks like she's teaching her pups to do the same. We need to start a fire."

chapter sixteen

"Northern Woods"

The **weary group** had now been walking for almost two full moons since the earth shake calamity destroyed their village, leaving the group of travelers no alternative than to seek another home. Between the fissure and the flood nearly every family had loved ones that had passed over to the Spirit World. People were beginning to question the validity of continuing the journey north. They had recently passed through a beautiful valley with a small stream feeding a lake. Traveler and Emma had both ignored the pleas of a few to at least take a closer look at the valley.

Traveler was convinced they were getting close to the location of the village and the boy he sought. For one thing, he noticed the temperature was becoming cooler. He vaguely remembered this drop in temperature the first time he had visited the village. However, a second event occurred which reinforced his conviction that the village was getting near. Early that vary morning, just before first light, he was visited by the night vision of a tall, sandy haired boy. The encounter was very fleeting. The shadow vision briefly materialized from the morning mist, a tall boy standing and beckoning in the middle of a forest trail, before quickly stepping away to vanish in the surrounding shadows.

Emma was sitting beside him around the morning fire, as thin pieces of the morning's ratta sizzled on green sticks over the coals. As usual, Onyx, and Violeta were sitting nearby, watching their youngsters playing tag with the pups.

"I had a shadow vision visit my dreams this morning," he mentioned to Emma as they nibbled on dried berries and nuts, waiting for the meat to cook.

"A tall boy in the woods?" She asked.

"The same," Traveler replied, no longer shocked by Emma's ability. He cut off a piece of raw ratta and tossed it in Scar's direction. She snatched the offering from mid-air, and rose to a sitting position, watching Traveler intently.

"I've been dream-walking with this spirit for the past handful of nights," the young girl said matter-of-factly. "I've been wondering if or when you might receive a visit."

The old man stopped cutting up bits of ratta and stared at the girl in disbelief. "Why didn't you say something?"

She smiled back at him, nodding her head. "I didn't want to interfere with your dreams." She looked to the grassy area the kids and pups were playing before adding, "Your visions are strong. Much stronger than you thought."

They turned their attention to the children that had gathered to chase one pup after another. Onyx and Violeta's two kids led the attack. The pups would lay still in the grass before darting away at the last moment as the kids reached out trying to touch them.

Traveler thought back to the days of his first encounter with the isolated village they now sought. He was unaware a village even existed this far north. It was the only time he had ever visited the village, and it was totally by accident. Or at least that's what he thought at the time.

Traveler was trying to find another animal similar to the one he had seen journeying with his father in his youth. He was lost in the far northern forest when he stumbled upon a faint trail. He saw various animal tracks in the muddy trail; none of which recognized. He thought he was looking at a game trail so he was somewhat surprised when he spotted human tracks as well. Under the circumstances, it was an easy decision to follow the trail, and he eventually came to a small village.

With all the shadow visions Traveler had been having nightly, the old man was now convinced it was not by accident that he had arrived at this village. He was certain, Mother Earth was somehow directing his path forward.

That had been Traveler's first time visiting the village and speaking with the young, sandy haired, miracle boy. He remembered that the boy's name was Jim. He had been certain even back then, that it would not be his last visit with Jim.

A runner, sent out from the village, located Traveler's group in late afternoon. Traveler and Emma were discussing which way to go as the weary villagers rested around them. Scar was first to alert the group of possible danger when she suddenly rose and gave her warning with a low guttural growl. Instantly, her four pups jumped up to join in with low growls of their own. The men, along with a few women, quickly formed a defensive ring around the children and aged, spears in hand. This was not the first time Scar and her pups had alerted the party of a marauding animal since they have entered this northern forest.

"Hello, Traveler!" a call came from the direction the animals all faced. "Do you control your beasts? Is it safe to come in?" the stranger yelled out.

"You may come!" Traveler yelled back.

The old man quickly turned to Scar and held his hand in front of her head as he said, "Friend." Scar stopped growling and dropped down to her belly. Three of the pups followed their mother's lead, and dropped down as well. Emma's big male did not. He moved over to remain standing next to Emma.

The stranger cautiously emerged from the forest and slowly approached the group.

"Are you sure your gullies won't attack?" the stranger asked.

"As long as they don't see you as a threat, you'll be safe," Traveler replied. "Why do you call 'em gullies?"

"Cause that's their name," the stranger replied. "Why? What do you call 'em where you come from?"

"We've never seen 'em before. Leastways, not in the South where we lived."

"We occasionally hunt 'em here," the visitor replied, quickly adding. "Only the bad ones that kill our schem. The good ones kill the ratta, so it's sort of a compromise; a trade off so to speak. The gullies are rather tasty though, and their hide makes fine leather. "

"Well, we've become rather attached to these gullies, so no more talk of killing 'em," the old man stated. "How did you know my name and how did you know we were here?"

"Jim sent me to guide you in. It's easy to get lost in the woods. My name's Pip, by the way," the young boy stated. "Jim knew you were getting near from his dreams. He and Emma have been in touch now for a long time. If we leave now, we can reach the village before night fall."

Traveler had previously left the village with many questions left unanswered. He had promised Jim when he had left that he would search for a suitable mate and promised to return if he found one. He was growing excited with the thought of introducing Emma in person.

chapter seventeen

"View From Above"

"**Sir, I think they spotted the floater,**" said the young Gloke officer sitting in front of the monitor speaking from the smaller of his two heads. Both heads continued to study the monitor, not turning to address their superior officer. "The old man is pointing at it with the boy."

"We predicted they would eventually," the Chief Gurd hissed, turning one of his reptilian yellow eyes in the Gloke's direction. "I am surprised though that it took them that long to spot. It shouldn't change anything, though. They have no idea what they're looking at. As far as they're concerned it could be a slider."

"Sir, I don't think they have any sliders on this planet."

"That's my point, idiot," the Chief Gurd hissed in reply.

"But, …" The smaller headed Gloke started to reply, before thinking better of it.

"They probably think it's some sort of insect. They should eventually ignore it if they don't feel threatened. After all, humans are an inferior race. The important question now is are they still moving north?" he asked the young officer.

"No, they are currently resting in the boy's village," the larger Gloke head replied sharply, turning to address his superior officer while the smaller head continued to study the monitors.

"Did you send them the image of the beautiful river with the animal herds running in the meadow?" the reptilian creature asked.

"We did as you ordered, sir, but I think that might have scared them."

"How could such a beautiful image scare them?" the Chief Gurd asked. "I made that image myself."

"Well, sir, the image didn't have any trees," replied the larger head. "They shelter in the trees at night."

"Plus, they have no way of knowing if those animals are a threat," added the smaller head.

"Well, take out the animals and put in some trees, and send it again!" the Chief Gurd hissed angrily, not wanting to admit to his mistake.

"More to the point, do you think they're gonna make it to the ship in time?" the Chief Gurd asked before hissing.

"Not if they stay much longer where they are now, no, I'm afraid not. This human species is weaker than most. I think they'll just sit there and rest."

"Then find a way to speed them up!" the Chief Gurd yelled, hissing loudly. The scales on the back of his neck and head began to rise and grow darker, his anger raising. "If they miss the ship, they'll miss the jump. If they miss the jump, heads will roll; and it won't be mine! All the other humans the Intergalactic Supreme Council wanted off this doomed planet are already in place. Everybody's just waiting on us!"

"We could destroy this village with another ground shake, like we did with the other one?" the smaller head quickly suggested.

"That's not gonna happen. The last time you two fools tried that, you put the girl in serious danger and came close to drowning the old man. We can't risk losing either. Nor the boy, for that matter. The Supreme Council insists they need them all," the Chief Gurd's voice hissed loudly in reply. "Somehow, the council has come to the conclusion this crazy human sub-species is deserving of another chance."

"I still don't understand how the old man can be of any use in their resettlement program? I would think, he'd probably die in hyper-sleep transport," the larger head stated.

"It's not your place to question the ISC's decisions, but if I had to guess, they're going to try to rejuvenate him," the Chief Gurd hissed in reply. "I heard one of the droids say he'll be a new man once he's rejuvenated. The council seems to think he's some kind of natural leader. Rejuvenation might work, but then again, it's never been attempted on such a low life form before."

"What a waste of good energy," the smaller head viewing the monitor muttered. "And, just think of the credits it will cost!"

"I suggest you keep your comments about the ISC's decisions to yourselves, and concentrate on getting these stragglers to the ship on time," the Chief Gurd hissed. "You might lose the second one of your puny heads if you fail."

"No! Please. Take the first head," the larger of the two heads immediately pleaded.

"Shut up!" the smaller head yelled.

The Chief Gurd ignored the Gloke's pleas, hissing back a warning before staring at him with a number of his yellow eyes. The tension in the ship was definitely rising.

"Does the council really think they'll just walk into an interstellar space ship once they arrive?" the young officer's smaller head watching the Chief Gurd sarcastically asked.

"If I had to guess," the Chief Gurd hissed in reply, "the floaters will gas them first when they get near enough and then the droids will move in to select the ones they want. The rest will be left behind. Their inferior brains will have their memories wiped clean before placing them in hyper-sleep for the jump. Jumps tend to be more successful with lower brain activity. Once they reach XB-503, the process will be reversed. Their brains will be downloaded with new memories and all the necessary information needed to survive on their new planet. The only thing they should remember from their previous life are their names. From past experience, names are the hardest thing to erase anyway, so the techs don't even bother trying any longer."

"From what I've been told," the smaller head said, "XB-503 is fairly similar to this planet, albeit a little colder. Plenty of water and oxygen, so they should do well. That is, of course, if they can somehow keep from killing each other."

The larger head added, "The Skul had been terraforming XB-503 for the last tolop period of time. I heard they even moved the planet nearer to a small star. That had never been accomplished before so they're understandably upset the council asked the Empress Cristina to take it away from them with a simple galaxy claim. Especially after moving the planet combined with the time and work they've invested in making it habitable."

"I don't blame them for being angry, but I'm sure they were well compensated with credits. They already control too many planets anyway, as far as I'm concerned," said the smaller head viewing the monitor.

When nobody responded, he continued, "I'm really lookin' forward to watching this planet's demise. I heard the DRP will be testing some sort of new sun-energy weapon."

"That's what I've heard as well. It should be quite a show," the Chief Gurd hissed. "But for now, let's just focus on getting these humans where they need to be or none of us will be around to enjoy it."

After a moment's thought, the larger head watching the Chief Gurd suggested, "Maybe a small forest fire would do the trick to get 'em moving again?"

After a short pause to consider the idea, the Chief Gurd hissed his reply. "That might actually work. Make it so," the reptile directed the smaller head controlling the monitor.

"Before I forget, though," the Chief Gurd asked, "have either one of you figured out just what a 'bird' is yet? The Emperor, for some unknown reason, really wants the old man to have birds on XB-503. As far as I know, no other planet in the known universe has a sub-species similar to what these humans refer to as a 'bird'. Right now we only have their stories as a reference point to guide us."

"We've both been searching and the only image the techs have been able to locate so far, that we think might be a bird, was on one side of some gold and silver trade tokens. Comparing the tokens to the bird on the walking staff the old man carries, it could be a bird, although much larger. Engraved on a metal strip attached to the bag containing the tokens, were two words. With the first word the techs could only recover the first two symbols; Am. However, the second word, the techs are pretty certain, are the five symbols; Eagle. They think the symbols refer to the animal on the token. We think the creature is a bird, an eagle. The problem we're facing now is the eagle's size. We can't seem to figure it out. We have no reference point to assist us that would show us just how big these damn eagles were. We don't even know how many legs they have!"

"Well, one of you two brains better come up with a solution fast!" the Chief Gurd hissed. "And remember, you can't be wrong if nobody else knows what's right. It's gonna take some time fabricating the number of eagles the ISC wants, and time's something we don't have to spare."

chapter eighteen

"XB-503"

Dawn came slowly over the land of Tolon. Only one of the three moons visible in the early morning sky was still high enough to give off any significant light. The other two were a dull purple, hanging low in the eastern sky. It would not be long before they joined their two sister moons that had already fled below the horizon sometime after midnight.

Having all five moons visible at the same time had been cause for celebration. None of the villagers could recall such an event ever happening before. That the High Priestess had somehow been able to predict it, was even more remarkable. The large majority of the villagers were convinced the five moons was a welcome sign from the Creator foretelling good fortune would befall the village. Perhaps foretelling of a good harvest or nice weather.

However, a few others saw the moons gathering together to gossip in the sky as a bad omen, a foreshadowing of an event of great consequence that was about to happen. They just couldn't agree on what that event might be.

Both groups gathered at The Bitter-Berry Tavern that evening. While the majority celebrated their good fortune and rejoiced far into the night with feasting, drinking, dancing, and singing, a few simply drank their concerns into oblivion.

The one remaining moon glowed a dull reddish-orange in the eastern sky as the sun finally broke through on the horizon to trigger a spectacular display of colors in the early morning mist. The night's dark lavender sky began to go through its usual array of pinks, oranges, and reds as the sun rose to prominence.

The bright morning rays of the small sun began to blaze through the cabin's only, heavily barred window to shine on Traveler's face. He squinted his eyes in response to the light and instinctively reached his hand up to his face. He often did this in reaction to stepping out into bright sunlight but he didn't know why. He pushed aside the heavy dish-hide robe that covered his body. The thick fur had laid warm against his nude body and the cold air of the cabin's interior made his body momentarily shudder.

Traveler slowly swung his legs around to sit on the bed's edge, allowing the cold air to wash over him as he stretched his muscular arms out above him. He had had the same dream again. The one with the girl with the crooked smile and sagging eye. She seemed so familiar, but he still couldn't place her in his memory. *'Who was she?'* He shook his head in frustration before rolling his head from side too side to loosen the kinks after the long night's slumber. His head ached from drinking too much bitter-berry wine in last night's celebration. He started to lean over with thoughts of gently shaking his mate from her slumber, but then thought better of it. It was probably best to let her sleep.

Traveler continued to sit on the side of the wooden bed a few more moments, rubbing the sleep from his eyes with both hands. When his mate, Amber, rolled away from the light and pulled the heavy robe over her head, Traveler grunted and stood. The cold air felt invigorating to his body, and the pounding in his head somewhat eased. For some unknown reason he throughly enjoyed the cold morning air. He pulled on his soft leather pants and shirt. Sitting on the bench by the table he pushed his feet into the fur-lined boots.

Moving over to the heavy pegs driven into the timber next to the door, he lifted his tish knife harness from one and secured it over his head and shoulder to allow the long blade's scabbard to rest at his side. He removed his thick tish leather vest from its peg and slipped it over his head, securing the three fastenings along its left side. The leather vest was elaborately decorated and signified Traveler's position as village chief. He didn't like wearing it, partly because of its weight, but also because of the responsibility it implied. He would much rather simply work with his eagles and be left alone. But, Amber insisted that he wear the vest, so he did so to please her. He grabbed his fur hat with the long fur ear flaps and pulled it down over his ears.

The last thing that Traveler reached over to grab was his walking staff. It leaned up against the wall next to the door. He always took his walking staff with him each time he stepped outside although he couldn't remember ever having a need to use it. He was told the walking staff had originally belonged to his grandfather, passed down through his father, but he wasn't really certain. Everybody said his father had been a mighty warrior but Traveler didn't remember him at all. In a drunken dare of courage his father had been killed fighting a tish when Traveler was only three.

Traveler unbolted the heavy wooden door's three iron bolts and stepped outside. As usual, Scar was standing there to greet him when he emerged. The big animal's snout was stained with blue so the young man knew she and her pack had been successful in their nightly hunt. As long as they left the scommer herds alone, he didn't care what they hunted. There certainly was no shortage of game to choose from. Blue-blooded brally certainly appeared to be last night's meal of choice.

Traveler looked above the distant snow-covered mountains to view the multi-colored light show of winter's dawn. Even though he had been watching this light show for the last twenty-eight winters, Traveler was still left in awe by its dazzling display. Almost as if it were his very first time viewing such beauty. Within a short time the brilliant colors faded, and the light lavender sky of winter was all that remained.

Due to the planet's slow rotation and long nights, heavy frost crunched under Traveler's boots on the gravel as he made his way down towards the big barn that housed the stables. As he walked he scanned the sky for clouds that might threaten snow, but he saw none. This assured the young man that within a very short time, the frost would vanish and the air would warm up dramatically. It was going to be a good day to fly. Given the choice between the two dominate seasons, Traveler would always pick winter over the stifling heat of summer.

Regardless of the season, Traveler needed to turn out the stable's eagles in order to feed. As he approached the huge barn that held the stables, Scar quickly trotted over to stand in front of the enormous doors. The big birds locked inside could easily be heard screeching and challenging each other through the barn door's thick planking.

"Stay away from the eaglets!" the young man warned Scar, already questioning in his mind if she would comply. Scar generally did whatever she wanted.

Traveler pointed his walking staff in Scar's direction and sternly said, "No!" Scar sank down onto her belly and watched, as he turned to pick up the wooden mallet laying nearby. He used it to knock the heavy iron locking pins from their holes and tossed the mallet aside. He then lifted the two logs that secured the wide barn doors in place from the outside. If somehow the giant eagles were to break out of their cages, they would still have a difficult time breaking through these heavy doors.

Scar beat him to the small, thick, man-door located nearby. As Traveler opened the small door, Scar pushed her way past him before he had a chance to walk in. Once inside, he quickly closed the heavy man-door behind him. He already had one eagle fledgling rush by him to escape in the past, and was determined it would never happen again. Dim, dusty light filtered down to the cages below from small, iron-barred, windows that ran along the top of the barn's walls. Once the door was closed, Traveler paused for a moment to allow his eyes to adjust to the dim light of the interior.

The large barn doors and the smaller man-door they had just entered were located in the center in the barn's long side wall. Twenty large cages lined the barn sides, ten on each side. The center of barn was left open so the giant eagles could easily walk down the center as they came and went through the central barn doors. Four of the cages stood empty while the others each held a mated pair of the huge birds. Traveler had recently sold four adult pairs since he now had new hatchlings to train. If all the chicks survived, which was highly unlikely, he would have to sell off some more pairs. That would be an unexpected plus, but for now it was better just to wait.

The two night shift stable hands quickly rose from their seats by the iron stove and called over in greeting as their boss entered. The two hands were siblings, a boy and a girl, and Traveler had just recently hired them from the orphanage. He wasn't looking to hire a girl, but Amber insisted they remain together. Each had slight deformities, which was not unusual amongst the local villagers, but Traveler felt they would not interfere with their duties.

"Good morn-n," Traveler greeted in return. "Sorry I'm late. It was quite the night of celebrating," he added as he walked over to warm himself by the iron stove. He set the walking staff aside and began warming his hands. After a few moments he asked, "Any problems during the night?"

"No, Sir," the two replied in unison.

"I think the eggs in the forth cage are begin'n to crack. Least that's what it sounded like to me," Candela added. "If that's the case, the eaglets should hatch by tomorrow night at the latest."

"Blessed be the Creator, that would make five pairs; quite a banner year," Traveler said. He wondered to himself whether the five moons could have played a part with the unusual number of eaglets. The longer he thought about it, the more he doubted it. *The High Priestess had envisioned something much bigger.*

"Have all the birds been watered?"

"Yes, sir!" Bohdie said.

"What about the cages?" Traveler asked. "You able to wash 'em all out?"

The two looked at each other a moment before Bohdie managed to reply. "They're all clean 'cept for six 'n seven. We tried Sir, but the birds wouldn't let us near. They both have new eaglets, 'n well, you know, we tried, but we couldn't get near 'em."

"You told us not to agitate 'em none," Candela interrupted, "so we thought it best to just leave 'em alone."

"That's OK, you did the right thing. I'll have Diego and Orion take care of 'em when they get here. You 'n your brother are just kinda new to 'em, that's all. You ain't earned their trust yet. It's just a matter of the amount of time you've been 'round 'em, that's all," Traveler replied before dismissing the two stable hands.

Candela paused before leaving. "Sir, do you mind if I ask you a question?"

"What's on your mind?" Traveler replied.

"It's about your walk'n staff," she said.

"What about it?"

"Well, I've looked at it a few times now, 'n I don't recognize what creature you have carved on the knob end. What is that?"

Traveler picked up the walking staff and looked at it again, as he had done many times in the past. "To be honest with you, Candela, I don't rightly know. In a strange sort of way it looks a little like an eaglet, but that's all I can tell you. It's missing the upper pair of claws, though. I know the staff once belonged to my grandfather, but perhaps it could be much older. It's hard to tell what creatures there might have been in the years past."

"It sure is interesting to look at. I think you may be right, it's probably related to our eagles," the girl answered.

"Very well could be. You two head on down to the cookhouse 'n get some breakfast," Traveler said, setting the walking staff aside. "And, I want you to know, I'm sorry you kids had to miss out on last night's celebration. Ask Joe if he has any cake left over, or something. Make sure to tell 'im I told you to ask. I may not be back when you return tonight, but you seem to know the routine."

The eagles all watched as the two stable hands pushed open the man-door and walked out, closing the door behind them. The eagles quickly shifted their attention to Traveler as he prepared to make his daily walk around the cavernous barn. He lay his staff by the fire before unbuckling and removing the leather vest, dropping it by the staff. Grabbing the meat bag hanging on a peg in the wall, Traveler was pleased to see the bag was full of fist size chunks of dunt meat. Keeping the meat bag full was part of the stable hand's duties, but it occasionally was forgotten.

Looping the heavy bag over one of his shoulders, Traveler began to walk down one side of the big barn and back the other. Scar walked at his side. He briefly stopped in front of each giant cage and spoke to each eagle in turn, calling each bird by name. As he spoke quietly to each, he tossed them a chunk of meat which they easily caught with their upper, smaller, pair of claws.

Four of the cages Traveler stopped in front of had eaglets of various sizes poking their heads out from under a sitting parent. It was obvious from the stench, that cages six and seven still needed attention, so he didn't linger long in front of either of them. After he completed his inspection, he returned to begin his work at cage number one. Since it was occupied by adult birds, the cage had little odor. Adult eagles relieved themselves as they flew, never in their cages.

Traveler unlocked the cage and stepped in, closing the heavy cage door behind him. He walked over to the smaller of the two eagles perched on their thick hind legs side by side on the elevated log. He greeted the eagle by name and continued to distract him with talk and a chunk of meat as he clipped the free end of a heavily braided line to the iron ring attached to the eagle's heavy lower leg before quickly stepping back. The other end of the braided line was already secured to the wall ring.

Traveler then pushed open the cage door, stepped through the door and called the untethered bird out. As usual, both of the caged eagles attempted to follow him, but the smaller eagle was abruptly stopped by the braided line secured to the ring on his leg.

"Moon Glow will be back shortly, Midnight," the young man said as he tossed the black bird a second chunk of meat. Midnight protested once with a loud screech before stepping back onto the log perch in the cage to tear at the meat with his beak. Traveler closed and secured the cage door behind him and returned his attention to the big eagle waiting patiently in the central isle.

The eagle was Traveler's own personal mount, and he had named her, Moon Glow. Besides being larger than her all-black mate, Moon Glow was easily the largest bird in the stables. Most of her body was covered with orange brown flaps of soft material known to all as leathers. As far as Traveler remembered he was the first person to refer to them as *'leathers'*. He didn't remember where he heard the term but it just felt appropriate.

Moon Glow's head and neck were covered with fine, white head leathers and she had a beautiful orange brown trace of leathers flowing across the top edge of her long wing leathers. This orange brown trace and her lighter body leathers seemed to change colors as the sun light played over them, similar in shade to Tolon's biggest moon.

The giant bird patiently followed Traveler down the central isle, stooped over, occasionally walking on all four of her legs, while screeching at each cage she passed, before walking out through the wide barn doors. Once they had passed outside he called out the bird's name again followed by the command to "stay". The eagle settled down on all four of her legs, shaking her white head leathers side to side, but she did not move. Traveler turned and quickly secured the large doors behind them.

"I know, I know; you want to eat." Traveler lovingly rubbed the bird's huge hooked beak and stroked the brown leathery flaps on Moon Glow's chest, before stepping back and commanding, "Up, up, up!"

Moon Glow immediately rose up and jumped high into the air using her powerful back legs and was soon out of the young man's sight. Traveler was well aware of where the eagle was headed, though. She was headed for the nearby Dumbie Sea to hunt her favorite food, dunt. It was hard to suggest it was really a hunt though. Dunt were so incredibly numerous along the Dumbie Sea's coastal islands and wide sandy beaches that it was easy pickings for the eagles. Especially since the dunt had no fear, what so ever, of the big birds. Even when the eagles landed amongst them, the dunt remained perfectly still, continuing to sun themselves as the eagles hopped between them to select their meal.

Traveler knew Moon Glow would quickly gorge herself before returning to her mate at the stables. Midnight would then have his opportunity to eat. The leg restraints would be quickly reversed, and the process would be repeated. At all times, unless having a rider, one of the mated eagles would remain secure in the stables. If a mated pair were allowed out of the stables at the same time, there was a great risk they would not return.

The only deviance from this simple routine involved eagles with young eaglets. When those eagles returned from their hunt, they would disgorge the chunks of dunt they had eaten directly into the mouths of their ravenous eaglets. Each pair of eagles with eaglets were then allowed the opportunity to hunt a second time. As the eaglets grew older, their parents began to bring the entire dunt's carcass back to the stables, grasped in their talons. They usually clutched one or more of the small dunt with each of their four taloned feet.

Traveler had released the first eagle from the third cage and was beginning to wonder what happened to the daytime stable boys, when Diego and Orion entered through the small man-door on the end of the barn.

"Thought for a bit there, you lads were't coming," Traveler called over sarcastically. He then thought to himself it was hard being angry when he had been late himself.

"Sorry Boss, hard night." Diego said.

"I hear yeah there," Traveler responded. "You two can start with cages six and seven."

"Will do."

"The eagles didn't let the new stable hands near on account of the newly hatched eaglets," Traveler said. "If you release one of the birds I think you'll be able to clean up the eaglets' crap. Be sure you take the meat bag with you, and be generous with the chunks as you clean. If you work fast, you should be able to clean the cage before the first bird gets back. And, make sure they have fresh water."

As Traveler returned to cage number four, all the eagles still in the stables started screeching loudly, demanding their breakfast. Their screeching protest reverberated throughout the huge barn. Even though they were all tame, and had never been known to harm a human, a stranger might question that idea if one of the giant eagles screeched in their face. Each of the eagles were easily the height of three humans and were very intimidating the first time a person approached one.

Traveler was a breeder of eagles and trained each of the adults to carry a human on their back. The training process generally took three to five cycles depending on both the eagle and rider's temperament. The stable of eagles and the two flocks of scommer were Traveler and Amber's total source of trade tokens.

Diego and Orion were each in the process of leading the second eagles from cages six and seven out through the big barn doors when they ran into Traveler coming the other way. Traveler was leading one of the returning eagles from cage three. After he secured the eagle in his cage, Traveler decided to check on how much progress the boys had made with cages six and seven. He was pleased to see the first two eagles had already returned, fed their eaglets and were waiting patiently for the two stable boys to walk them out to feed again. Both cages had been throughly cleaned and washed down with water and a thick stable broom.

"Nice work, lads. Did they give you any trouble?" Traveler said as the two boys were returning.

"No, Sir," Orion replied.

"It appears to me, I'm no longer needed here. You two seem to be able to handle the eagles quite nicely," Traveler said. "I'm gonna head up to the North Bay scommer herd. The boys are doing the winter cut'n and I heard a report of a big tish being spotted in the area. I think it best I go and check it out. I don't want to lose any of the scommer, or for that matter, any herders either if I can help it."

"Sounds good, Sir. Diego and I can handle things here," Orion replied. "I was about ready to ask you anyway, Sir, if Diego can head up to the cookhouse for his mid-morning meal?"

"That's fine, but be sure to take Scar with you when you walk about. This is the time of year you want to be extra alert with all the tish marauding about," Traveler warned.

Traveler called Scar over and told her to go with Diego, and the two immediately left in the direction of the cookhouse.

Turning back to Orion, Traveler said, "Be ready with the barn doors when I walk Moon Glow out. She'll have the spurs on and I'm not quite sure how she'll react."

"Yes, Sir," Orion responded.

Traveler put on his leather vest with the heavy fur collar before he returned to the first cage and called Moon Glow over. "Do you want to fly?" Of course he already knew the answer. The big bird began excitedly hopping from one foot to the other, her upper legs moving rapidly back and forth, almost in a clapping motion.

He tossed Midnight a chunk of meat before quickly clipping his lower leg to the wall ring. He then opened the wooden case nailed to the wall and pulled out one of the long, iron spurs from within. Traveler had recently designed the two deadly spurs and the blacksmith had custom made them to fit over the curved talons on each of Moon Glow's upper leg middle toes. The big bird watched and waited patiently on the log while Traveler secured the spurs in place and tied them with a leather strip to the back of the eagle's own talons. The spurs were twice the length of her own upper talons and razor sharp.

If they were going to hunt tish together Traveler wanted to have a clear advantage. He was certain the long iron spurs would give Moon Glow just such an edge if he could somehow train her how to use them. But he was also concerned that she accidentally might cut herself. This was the first time she wore them, and he was happy to see she wasn't moving them about much.

Moon Glow followed Traveler as he walked down the central isle and out the big barn doors Orion had opened. Traveler was pleased to see the eagle walking on her back feet instead of all fours. She must not trust the long talons with her weight.

"Good hunting," Orion yelled over the screeching from within as Traveler and Moon Glow exited the barn.

As soon as Moon Glow had cleared the barn doors, Traveler yelled, "Down, down," and the big bird squatted as before, lowering her head almost to the ground.

Traveler stepped onto the eagle's front claw. He grabbed a fistful of neck leathers in his left hand, and threw his right leg over her neck. As trained, Moon Glow assisted him by lifting the front claw he was standing on. Once she felt Traveler sitting on her shoulders, the big bird immediately stood up on her powerful hind legs. As Traveler adjusted his position on her shoulders he could feel her muscular shoulder muscles move below him, anticipating his next command. He bent his lower legs below her wings and shifted his handholds to grasp a fistful of neck leathers and reins on either side of Moon Glow's neck. Leaning forward, Traveler commanded, "Up, up, up!" and the huge eagle leapt straight up, as he held tight to her neck leathers.

When Moon Glow leveled off, high above the ground and began to glide on the warm air currents, she began to kick out with one front foot after the other in a futile attempt to dislodge the heavy spurs.

"Easy Moon Glow, it's OK," Traveler whispered beside her head, trying to calm her down. After a few more unsuccessful attempts to dislodge the spurs, the big eagle seemed to accept her fate and just ignored them all together. Traveler used pressure from his knees and hands full of neck leathers to turn the giant bird in the direction he wanted.

Once Traveler arrived above North Bay, it didn't take him long to locate the scommer herd. They were bunched together within temporary brush fences waiting to be cut. He scouted the area all around the herd in search of any tish, but was unable to see any. That didn't necessarily mean there were't any, but Traveler was somewhat relieved.

Moon Glow landed near the enclosed herd of scommer and Traveler slid down her wing to dismount. "Stay," he commanded Moon Glow and the big bird relaxed into a squatting position on all fours and began to groom herself with her beak.

Traveler walked over to the herders who were working on cutting the scommer that had been born in the spring. They were now old enough to have their tails bobbed and Traveler's distinctive notching cut into their ears. The 'long-tails,' as the herders referred to the uncut scommer, were easy to spot within the herd by their long, hairless tails. Young herders located the long-tails and walked them over to the cutters. The passive animals were led to the cutters with one hand on their single horn and the other gripping their tails.

Two cutters, working together, would complete the cuttings within seconds. One cutter quickly made two cuts at the base of the ear and one at the very top. At the same time this was being done, the other cutter lopped off the scommer's long tail at its base. The cut scommer were then released outside the brush walls to rejoin the herd. The small cuts would heal along the cut edges, easily denoting Traveler's ownership.

"We should be finished by nightfall," the head herder told Traveler as they watched the cutters and herders work.

"You gonna do the cut'n on the other herd too?" Traveler asked.

"No," the head herder replied. "I'm sure Jim can handle it. He's young 'n I don't wanna look like I'm try'n to show 'im up."

"Makes sense," Traveler replied. "I'll let you get back to work. I'm gonna fly around a little longer and see if I might spot that big tish people were talk'n 'bout."

"Good hunt'n, Boss, be careful."

Traveler remounted Moon Glow and he began to throughly search the area all around the North Bay. They flew over lots of game, from dunt, thick all along the coast, to large herds of brally and wild scommer. He saw no reason for a big tish to attack a small guarded herd of scommer with so much other game to be had. He was disappointed that Moon Glow was not going to have a chance to use the spurs, but it was good to let her get accustomed to flying with them on.

"Home, girl, home," Traveler yelled and she responded with a slow gliding turn to the South. Moon Glow gave a few heavy beats of her wings and the big bird surged forward. Traveler held on tighter to her neck leathers as the eagle's wings continued to beat.

Not much time passed before a dark spec appeared in the distant sky. It was flying their way, and closing the distance fast. Traveler soon became certain that the eagle coming his way was Midnight and that meant Amber was riding. Traveler immediately sensed trouble, since Amber had told him late last night she did not intend to fly today.

As the two eagles closed the gap between them, Traveler's guess was confirmed; it was Midnight and Amber. As Midnight flew by, Traveler heard Amber yell something. Unfortunately, both eagles screeched there greetings at the same moment and he did not understand her message. Midnight made a big sweeping turn and flew up alongside his mate.

"Big trouble, home!" Amber yelled. As soon as Traveler nodded his head in understanding, Amber kicked Midnight under the wings, urging him to fly faster. The big bird responded by surging forward.

Traveler nudged his heels against Moon Glow's side, and the big eagle easily began to gain on her mate. It wasn't long before they were landing beside the stable barn's big doors.

chapter nineteen

"Trouble"

"Thanks be to the Creator,** I was able to find you so quickly," Amber said as she slid down Midnight's wing to dismount. "There's been trouble down at the Bitter-Berry Tavern. Colt Banner's waiting for you right now up at the house."

"What kind'a trouble?" Traveler called down from Moon Glow's back.

"Colt didn't go into any details, just that he needed to speak with you right away. Something about Emma," Amber replied. "But, see'n how angry he is, it's gotta be something' bad. He's got a lot of men with 'im, 'n they're all wearing their blades."

"Well, it is tish season. You'd be foolish not to wear your blade. We're wearing ours."

Diego and Orion were waiting at the stable doors when they arrived, and Traveler instructed Diego to take Midnight back to his cage. Traveler remained on Moon Glow's back until Diego and Midnight disappeared inside the stable barn's doors. Amber didn't wait for Traveler but immediately turned and set out for their home.

Once Midnight was safely inside, Traveler slid down Moon Glow's wing and told the big eagle, "go home." She obediently followed Orion through the open barn doors. Traveler quickly closed and secured the big doors before turning and jogging to catch up with Amber. As they walked up the rise to their house, they could easily see a large crowd had gathered outside. A few of those gathered were his own hired hands, but others he did not know by name. He spotted Colt Banner standing by his door with his two oldest boys and hurried over.

"I fear your visit is not for pleasure," Traveler said as he approached, extending his hand to Colt.

"Nay, I'm 'fraid not, more of an official visit," Colt Banner replied as he shook Traveler's hand. "Some of it concerns your goddaughter, Emma."

"Let's step into the house 'n get away from pry'n ears."

Traveler led Colt and his two oldest boys into the house, shaking Gray and Caden's hands as they entered. Amber quickly closed the heavy door behind them. Traveler cleared the bench by tossing some furs in the corner and offered Colt Banner a place to sit down. Colt shook his head, choosing to remain standing, cap in hand.

"Now, what's that you say about Emma? Is she not with Jim, round'n up the scommer for tomorrow's cut'n?" Traveler asked, remaining standing himself.

"I'm afraid not, Traveler. That animal that stays by her side staggered into the house today, shortly after the mid day meal," Colt said. "I think Emma calls it Peeps, or Pete, or something like that. Anyway, the animal was all covered in blood, and I think most of it was his. Hurt real bad he was, tish claw wounds all over his body. It was obvious he wanted us to follow 'im, so I sent Gray 'n Caden. Gray, tell Traveler what you found."

"Well, the animal led us to the woods, east of town. You know, near the path leading to Bay Town," Gray said. "We found a real bloody mess all right. Bodies scattered everywhere. Emma was lying on the ground beside the body of our brother, Cooper. Jim was stuck up in a tree, unconscious. Emma and Jim were still alive, but barely."

"It was obvious a real struggle had taken place there," Gray said. "Nearby, we also found the body of one of 'em slant-eyes. He'd been stabbed in the chest."

"There was a big tish lying there dead as well, right in the middle of everything. He was surrounded by the other three dead animals of Emma's pack," Gray continued. "Damnedest thing then happened.

Peeps lay down beside Emma, put a big paw on her, and just closed his eyes 'n died. Died right there beside her after coming all that way 'n back to fetch us!"

"That crazy animal used every last bit of his energy to come 'n get help," Caden said. "We carried Emma 'n Jim back, since they were the only ones still alive. Emma kept repeat'n big 'tish, big tish' as I carried her, but she was really out of it."

"When Caden brought her into the house and lay her down on the bed she became hysterical. It took sometime for my Violeta 'n the maid to calm her down enough to where we could make any sense out of what she was saying," Colt Banner added.

Amber stood up from her seat on the edge of the bed to ask, "Is she gonna be all right? Is Emma OK?"

"I think so, but it's gonna take some time," Colt replied. "Besides be'n badly beaten, I think she was also violated; probably by more than one of 'em slant-eye bastards. That's gonna take a mite longer to heal."

"Emma was in 'n out of consciousness," Violeta told me. "Emma kept trying to tell us where to find Jim 'n Cooper, but of course we already knew. she kept say'n 'tish, tish' like a warn'n. I had the maid make her some herb tea to help ease her pain and help her rest."

Colt's eyes began to tear up as he continued. "The worst of it still remains the same! 'em slant-eyes killed my boy, Cooper, 'n beat Jim 'n Emma so bad they'll be lucky to pull through."

"How could all of this happen? We were all together down at the Bitter-Berry Tavern last night, celebrating with everybody else," traveler quietly said under his breath. "Amber and I left early but everybody seemed to be happy at the time. Certainly wasn't any sign of no trouble. Did anybody actually see what happened?"

"Caden, tell Traveler what you told me earlier," his father directed.

Colt's oldest son stepped forward a half step to answer. "Well, sir, the slant-eyes arrived late. I'm sure it was after you 'n Amber left. Cooper was already pretty drunk by that time 'n had words with one of 'em. I don't know what was said but Cooper challenged 'im to a fight. The man told Cooper he didn't want to fight, 'especially not a drunk.' My brother took a step toward 'im 'n the man pushed Cooper away hard. Cooper stumbled 'n fell over a bench, landing hard on his butt. The slant-eyes watch'n started laughing."

Caden continued, "You all know how Cooper is; loud 'n all. He didn't like 'em laughing 'n all, 'n started yell'n threats 'n stuff towards all 'em slant-eyes. Anyway, Gray 'n me stepped in 'n pulled 'im away. We both told Cooper to go home 'n sleep it off; that nobody wanted any trouble on such an important night. I knew Emma 'n Jim don't drink none, so I asked 'em if they would walk with Cooper. You know, stay with 'im; make sure he gets home 'n all. I figured with all the folks out celebrating 'n all, it would be safe enough walk'n through town."

"We should've gone with 'im," Gray quietly said under his breath. He repeated his words again, a little louder. "I told you last night, Caden, we should've gone with 'im. None of this would'a happened if we had just gone with 'im."

"Where did you say you found Emma, Jim, 'n Cooper?" Traveler asked the brothers, ignoring Gray's remarks.

"We found 'em in the woods east of the Bitter-Berry," Gray replied.

"That's quite a ways off the beaten path for get'n home," Traveler said. "Any idea how they ended up there?"

"'Em slant-eyes undoubtedly jumped 'em 'n took 'em there to beat 'em," Colt angrily stated. "The boys found Jim, beaten unconscious 'n stuck up in a tree. Cooper's body was mauled by the big tish, but he had also been badly beaten and stabbed multiple times. The dead tish lay in the center of everything. It looked pretty obvious that it was killed by Emma's pack of animals."

"Did you find Cooper's tish blade?" Traveler asked.

"No, but we were't look'n for it none either," Colt replied angrily. "When I returned to retrieve Cooper's body, the slant-eyes body was missing."

"What difference does his blade make?" Colt asked. "'Em slant-eyes probably took Cooper's blade when they fled from the tish. How do I know what happened to his blade. All I know is we're take'n the eagles 'n punish'n those slant-eyes first thing on the morn. The big question

I want to know, Traveler, is will you fly to Bay Town with us or not?" Colt asked. "You have the most eagles 'n we plan to stone the bastards from above."

"I think you're all jump'n to conclusions a might quick," Amber interjected. "There're too many questions still unanswered. Why did the Bay Town men wait so long before retrieving their friend's body? Perhaps we should try to talk with 'em first or at the very least wait to hear what Emma or Jim can tell us when they wake up."

"I think Amber's right," Traveler answered. "We should be certain of the facts before we go off stone'n a whole village for what a few individuals might've done. Amber 'n I will go with you now to your place Colt, to help Violeta care for Emma 'n Jim. Maybe when they wake they can shed some more light on exactly what happened. I also have to go visit Bay Town to hear their side of the encounter. If it's true what you're now think'n then I'll fly with you, but not before then."

"I say, enough talk'n. They killed my boy!" Colt yelled. "What else do I need to know? You can't believe anything 'em slant-eyes say. This, along with the unsolved murders down at Kerby's less than two moons ago, calls for something to be done; 'n I aim to do it, with or without you."

⎯⎯⎯⎯⎯◇○⟳○◇⎯⎯⎯⎯⎯

Amber and Traveler started the long walk back to Colt Banner's place with the angry mob. Before they left, Traveler told his own workmen who had gathered to get back to work. They turned to resume their chores. When the group arrived at the Banner farm, Colt told the men to return at sun up with their eagles and they too, quietly disbursed.

Traveler, Amber, and Violeta, took shifts sitting with the two injured young people. They offered what little comfort they could to Emma and Jim throughout the long night. Jim tossed and turned in his sleep, tormented by his dreams; often violently striking out and murmuring unintelligible words. He became feverish around midnight and Violeta brought out a clay water basin and rags to try to cool his body and lower his temperature. Jim's physical injuries appeared to be more severe than Emma's. He had been throughly beaten in the ordeal and was lucky to be alive. Although the group didn't think he had suffered any broken bones, they were very concerned about his head and possible internal injuries.

Violeta had already cleaned the numerous lacerations she had found on both victim's head and face before Amber and Traveler had arrived. She discreetly pulled Amber aside to tell her about her concerns with Emma bleeding from her female parts. She wasn't convinced Emma had been violated at all. She had tried to tell her husband, Colt, but he wouldn't listen. Violeta was almost certain the girl had endured a miscarriage instead.

"The poor child had been unable to say anything about her own ordeal except to tell 'em where to find Jim," Violeta told Amber. "She kept say'n to hurry. Repeat'n 'big tish, big tish,' over 'n over again as the herb tea started take'n effect."

The eagles and their riders began arriving way before sunrise the next morning. The men were all too willing to rain down their justice of stones on Bay Town, a new village of immigrants, for their perceived involvement in the recent killings. Some were already enhancing their courage by drinking bitter-berry wine from leather bags slung across their chests.

"We're gonna teach 'em slant-eyes not to mess with us! They need to understand once 'n for all, we don't want their kind here." Colt Banner yelled as he stepped out through the door to greet the men that had arrived. "We'll have the eagles pick up their stones at Cold Creek. That's pretty close to the slant-eye Bay Town."

As Colt started toward his eagle, being held by a stable hand, he called back to Traveler standing with Amber and Violeta by the house door.

"You sure you ain't changed your mind none, Traveler?"

"No," Traveler replied. "I still think you 'n your men should wait a spell. Jim's fever broke early this morn'n, 'n I think he'll wake up shortly. He might be able to shed some light on who did this. It might not even be the men from Bay Town. You all may be fix'n to make a terrible mistake. You lads shouldn't mind wait'n a bit, just to be sure."

"Pa, maybe Traveler's right," Gray softly said. "Maybe… ."

Colt Banner glared in his son's direction, cutting the boy off in mid sentence. Before any of the others that had gathered had a chance to consider Traveler's suggestion, the exasperated man yelled, "I ain't gonna wait no more! Words can't bring back my boy! Cooper demands justice now," before adding, "anyway, we already know the slant-eyes done it, don't we lads."

"Let's fly," Colt yelled as he climbed up to take his seat on the broad shoulders of his kneeling eagle.

Colt gave the eagle the command, "Up, up, up," and the big bird screeched as it jumped high and began to fly in the early dawn light. The group of men momentarily glanced around before rushing to mount their own eagles. Soon, all the great birds had vanished from view as they flew east; leaving Traveler, Amber, and Violeta standing at the Banner's doorstep.

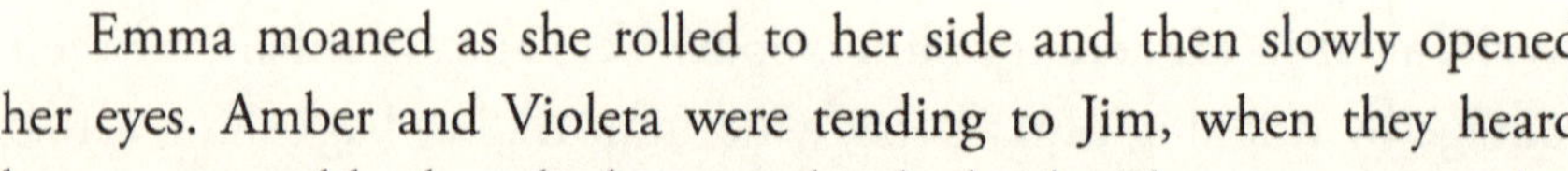

Emma moaned as she rolled to her side and then slowly opened her eyes. Amber and Violeta were tending to Jim, when they heard her moans and both rushed over to her bed-side. They were somewhat surprised because they had anticipated Jim being the first to wake.

"Praise be to the Creator, you've come back to us," Amber said softly, tears rushing to her eyes. "Don't try to move too much, Honey, you've been injured."

"Jim; is Jim OK?" Emma asked in a whisper. Her eyes slowly scanning the room around her. "Where am I, anyway?"

"You're safe dear, your at the Banner's," Amber answered, "And, Jim's here with you. I'll be right back, I'm gonna go 'n get Traveler."

Amber rushed out of the room to find Traveler, leaving Violeta by Emma's side. Within moments Amber and Traveler both rushed back in the room to stand by Violeta at Emma's side. Traveler gently took Emma's hand in his, before leaning forward to kiss her on her forehead.

"Blessed be the Creator," Traveler muttered quietly to himself. He gently squeezed Emma's hand, before saying, "Welcome back, Emma. Would you like a sip of water?"

When Emma nodded and struggled to raise her head from her pillow, Traveler gently assisted her with his hand behind her head. She opened her mouth to drink from the clay cup Amber held to her lips. She drank a few swallows before exhaustingly laying her head back on her pillow.

"How did I get here?" Emma asked.

"Peeps came 'n got help, that animal surely saved your life," Amber replied. "Don't you remember?"

"I vaguely remember being in a tree, but not much else." Emma took a deep, painful breath before asking, "I remember a big tish. Did Cooper or Jim kill the tish?"

"I'm sorry to say, Cooper didn't make it," Traveler answered. "He's dead."

"What about Peeps? Is he okay?"

"I'm afraid he's dead, too. The whole pack is dead. I'm sorry, Emma, I know how much you loved them." Traveler gently squeezed Emma's hand as he said the words.

Emma lay still for a long time, before a tear rolled down her cheek. Looking at Violeta she whispered, "I'm so sorry Violeta. We tried our best."

"I'm sure you did, my dear." Violeta said wiping a tear from her cheek.

"Can you tell us what happened after you left the Bitter-Berry Tavern?" Traveler asked.

Emma slowly nodded her head and began to tell her story. Her voice was soft and shaky as she tried to remember the previous night's horror.

"You guys had already left the tavern long before the fight. A small group of men 'n women from Bay Town were seated in the back of the tavern, celebrating 'n all, like the rest of us. Cooper saw 'em 'n tried to pick a fight with one of the men. At first the guy tried to ignore Cooper, which made Cooper even more belligerent. The man finally stood up and pushed Cooper away hard, saying he didn't want to fight no drunk. Cooper tripped over a bench and fell pretty hard. Everyone started laugh'n which made Cooper even angrier. Gray 'n Caden rushed over then 'n pulled their brother away."

"Caden tried to apologize to the man for his Cooper's behavior, but that made Cooper even crazier. He started yelling at his brothers then, Gray 'n Caden. I didn't exactly understand what he was yelling 'cause he was slurring his words 'n all, but he seemed pretty upset that his brothers didn't step in 'n help 'im fight the Bay Town men."

"I think it was Gray that then asked Jim 'n I if we would take Cooper home, on account of 'im being so drunk 'n all. We knew the Banner farm was on our way, so we said we'd be glad to. We didn't realize what we were getting into, with Cooper being so drunk. When we left the tavern he just wasn't himself. He was extremely angry 'n shout'n 'n stuff about how he wasn't gonna let 'em slant-eyes get away with making 'im look bad. That's what he called 'em fellas from Bay Town; slant-eyes. Jim 'n I tried to talk 'im down 'n take 'im home, but he refused to go. He kept on mumbling stuff about how no one's gonna push 'im 'round none 'n he'd show his brothers he could take care of 'imself. He turned around and headed east through the forest. You know, toward Bay Town. He was obsessed with teach'n 'em slant-eyes a lesson."

"I'm so sorry Violeta, but Cooper's a big guy, 'n Jim 'n I couldn't stop 'im." Emma began to softly weep as she continued. "We tried to talk 'im out of it, we surely did. He just wouldn't listen. He caught up to a group of men head'n towards Bay Town in the woods. They had just left the tavern and were heading home. I don't even think it was the same men from the tavern as before, on account of the fact I didn't see any women. But, that didn't seem to matter to Cooper."

"Everything happened so fast then. Before we could stop 'im, Cooper drew his tish blade, grabbed one of the men by the shoulder, 'n spun 'im around. Cooper yelled something at the man 'n just stabbed the man in the chest. Jim 'n I rushed forward to try to stop 'im, but it happened so fast we were too late."

"That sounds like something Cooper might do. Being the youngest, he always was a reckless 'n foolhardy boy," Violeta interjected. "He was very jealous of his older brothers, always try'n to impress 'em 'n all."

Emma continued, "After the stabbing the others jumped us 'n started to beat us. They probably thought Jim 'n I were siding with Cooper so they beat us pretty bad, too. I remember being knocked down and someone kicking me in my stomach. It hurt so bad I must have passed out."

"Were you pregnant, Emma?" Amber asked.

"I'm not sure, I think so. I wanted to be sure, so I haven't told Jim yet," Emma replied.

"I fear you've lost the baby," Amber said softly. "I'm pretty sure you've had a miscarriage."

Emma's eye opened wider as her hands moved to her stomach. Tears formed in her eyes and she turned her head to the wall.

"We probably should let her rest now," Amber suggested to the other two.

"Just a couple of more question," Traveler said. "Emma, do you remember climbing a tree? They found Jim up in a tree."

"No, but I vaguely remember being up in a tree as well. I don't know how I got there, though. The last thing I remember about last night was a fuzzy vision of a big tish standing over Cooper below the tree I was in. I could hear Cooper yelling, and fighting, but the tish was big 'n I'm not sure Cooper still had his tish blade. I think I tried to climb down to help, but I can't remember anything after that."

"When I woke up again, I remember seeing Caden standing over me. I don't remember anything else."

"That's enough talk'n for now," Amber said. "Try to get some rest, dear. And, remember Emma, none of this is you or Jim's fault; I ain't blaming you for any of it."

chapter twenty

"The Observers"

"I don't believe it. I don't believe how barbaric this human species is," one of the gray furred heads said to its partner. The Lapling's two heads were viewing the images projected on the fourth dimension observation square floating in the air in front of them.

"Look how violent they are," the other head replied. "I've never seen anything like it. They're using the very eagles Empress Cristina had engineered for them to help kill other humans!"

Both Lapling observers watched the projections in disgust as humans mounted on eagles rained down stones on the helpless villagers below.

"Yes, it is perplexing. Especially after all the time and resources the Intergalactic Supreme Council has invested in trying to salvage the species. All their efforts to cull this species of its violent nature, seem to be for naught," one of the heads on the spotted Lapling stated.

The gray furred Lapling agreed, as it unwound its tail from the ring it was hanging from. The suckers on its hind expenditures held it in place as it readjusted its tail.

"First the council gave them the atom for unlimited energy; and what did they do? They took this gift of knowledge to make bombs that destroyed their original planet. Then the council gave them a new planet, with abundant food and animals. Even engineering this creature they call an eagle for easy transportation. But, this sub-species turned that gift into a weapon to feed their violent nature and kill one another. It doesn't make any sense."

"You're right, of course, it doesn't. Make sure the ISC gets a recording of this," one of the spotted Lapling's heads directed.

"It's already happening," its partner responded. "The ISC's viewing the same projection as we speak."

"After the two senseless killings at that place they call Kerby's a short time ago, this massacre taking place now might very well lead to the extermination of this sub-species."

The gray furred Lapling's whiskers twitched as it nodded its heads in agreement. "I think you're right, something's inherently broken in their mental process. They can't seem to control their own thoughts. This pathetic species is fixated on emotions. It's in their DNA. Their emotions of superiority, hate, jealousy, and anger overrule any logic their meager brains have. Killing one another is simply the natural consequence of those emotions."

"They do it so easily," one of the spotted Lapling's heads stated. "Can you two imagine what would have happened if the Lapling's behaved like that? Killing members of our own specious simply over an emotion? I assure you, we would have been exterminated long ago."

"I wonder what the ISC is going to rule?" one of the gray Lapling heads asked.

"The Empress will probably go along with whatever the council decides; she usually does," it's partner replied.

"What's that idiom these human's use?" one of the two spotted Lapling heads asked.

"I think you might be thinking of their expression, 'It's a no-brainer!'" its partner answered. "Sounds appropriate."

"That's quite close to our old Lapling saying, 'there's no cure for stupid,'" one of the gray heads replied. "Either of you two spots want to lay a wager on what Empress Cristina's decision will be? We'll lay you three-to-one it's extermination.'""

Some time later:

"The Empress did what??!!!" One of the gray Laplings exclaimed, dumbfounded.

"That's hard to believe!" The gray's other head responded.

" I win!!!" The smallest spot exclaimed excitedly.

The End

a word from the author.

Thank you very much for purchasing my recent novel; *Traveler*. I'm sure you would also enjoy my first novel; **Spirit Bow, The Saga of Sean O'Malley.** Writing under my pen name of Grandpa Peeps, I am also proud to have published two wonderful children's books in verse, **The Squire and the White Dragon** and **How to Catch a Whopper.**

Since I am a little known author, I would greatly appreciate your help in getting the word out. There are two easy ways you can do this.

First, if you enjoyed the book, please post a short review on amazon. com, bookbaby.com, or citiofbooks.com. Positive reviews push books to the front of the line on these platforms.

Secondly, put a book recommendation out over your social media accounts to your friends.

Thanks again, sincerely,   James Lettis

spiritbow,thesagaofseano'malley
James Lettis

In November of 1819, young Sean O'Malley sets out on a fateful hunt with his grandfather and accidentally shoots a young Indian boy out on a vision quest. Grandpa says nothing can be done for the dying boy and takes the young Indian's Spirit Bow. Resentful of the local natives, Grandpa tells his grandson, "Nice shot." These simple words will haunt Sean for years to come. The young Indian's death sets in motion, a series of tragic consequences that will have a lasting effect on young O'Malley.

Sean blames himself for the tragedy that befalls his family and becomes convinced the bow's spirits are seeking their vengeance. As Sean and his father, Patrick, make their way toward Oregon Country they enlist the help of Patrick's sadistic half-brother, Jack, and his captive squaw, Chimalis. On their journey west, Sean and Patrick slowly learn of their family's dark past. Jack murders Patrick, blaming the Indians. Chimalis and Sean eventually escape Jack's evil clutches and through a strange twist of fate, Sean finds himself living among Chimalis's Crow Indians. While he is still haunted by past memories and his grandfather's words, "Nice shot," he slowly begins to find comfort and appreciation of the Indian's way of life. Over time Sean gains the respect of his new Crow family and friends. After saving his best friend's life, Sean earns his warrior name, Night Wind. Have the bow's spirits changed sides?

The inevitable conflict with white immigrants forces Night Wind to intervene as he tries to prevent a massacre and possible war the tribes cannot win. The after effects of his intervention change his life forever.

SPIRIT BOW

THE SAGA OF SEAN O'MALLEY

JAMES LETTIS